This volume of

REPRESENTING
SUPER DOLL

is especially for the readers

of

Healdsburg Public Library

With the Best Wishes

of

Richard Peck

October, 1977

Also by Richard Peck

Don't Look and It Won't Hurt
Dreamland Lake
Through a Brief Darkness

REPRESENTING SUPER DOLL

Richard Peck

THE VIKING PRESS NEW YORK

First Edition

Copyright © 1974 by Richard Peck
All rights reserved. First published in 1974 by
The Viking Press, Inc., 625 Madison Avenue,
New York, N.Y. 10022. Published simultaneously in
Canada by The Macmillan Company of Canada Limited.
Printed in U.S.A.   1   2   3   4   5   78   77   76   75   74

Library of Congress Cataloging in Publication Data

Peck, Richard. Representing Super Doll.
Summary: After being involved in the brittle
superficial world of a beauty contest, a country girl
appreciates even more the solid values of her Indiana
farm life. [1. Beauty contests—Fiction.
2. Family life—Fiction] I. Title. PZ7.P338Re
[Fic] 74–8690 ISBN 0–670–59492–x

For Velma and Burl Bauer

chapter

one

*M*ama came in off the back porch, and her hands were wringing wet with blood. She pushed the door open with her behind and made straight for the sink. "Turn those taps on for me, Verna, I'm drenched."

The blood swirled down the pipe, and a little puddle of pink water followed. I tried to keep my eyes down on the drain, but I knew I'd look up. And I knew what I'd see out the window.

On the square of grass where we stretch the clothesline there was a scattering of white feathers. I wanted to look back in the sink then, but I didn't. I just kept scanning the yard, squinting a little to keep from seeing too clear.

Then I saw the first one, wedged up against the cob house right along the line of marigolds. It was a chicken, still clawing the air. And where its head had been was a red nothing. It was flopping its last among the flowers.

twelve

I wasn't squinting then in spite of myself. The bright yellow marigold dust was powdering the feathers that weren't already messed with blood.

I knew there was another one. There always is. Mama kills one to fry and one to freeze. There it was, half in and half out of the first row of sweet corn in the garden. Since it was farther off, I couldn't see the blood. But it was twitching, and so was I.

Mama had turned toward the roller towel, but she can always read my mind, different as we are. She sighed her little sigh and said, "Looks like a farm girl would get used to certain sights and come to terms with them. It's what chickens are for."

I didn't much want to hear about the destiny of chickens. But Mama fell silent because we both heard Aunt Eunice start down the back stairs from her room. She always watches from her window while Mama deals with the chickens. She stands stock still up there, holding the curtains back and staring down until the heads are off and Mama walks down to the fence and flings them over to where the dogs can get at them.

I'm not saying I know why Aunt Eunice watches, but she always does. And Mama knows it. She often remarks on it.

Mama has her own way of killing. I only watched once, but I have a very clear mental picture. She has a horror of axes and never goes near one. Instead she'll grip a fat fryer by the neck and bring it out to the clothesline yard. It'll be fanning out and trying to work loose. But

Mama plants her feet apart right in the middle of the yard and screws up her face like its going to hurt her worse than the victim. Then she begins to swing the bird in big cartwheels at an angle over her head.

Mama's not a big woman, and along with Dad she's as gentle a human being as ever lived. But that first swing is a neckbreaker, which is a mercy for the chicken. She keeps whipping it around and around though, until the body parts company with the head and goes jumping and spreading feathers all over the yard. And that's the part I can't stomach. There's too much of the town girl in me, I guess. And maybe there always was.

The door next to the stove opened, and Aunt Eunice walked in. She had a lace hanky stuck down the front of her dress. And she said what she nearly always says. "The price of feed what it is, I don't know why you keep poultry, Edith. I don't see where it pays, let alone the bother and being tied down."

"I like to know where my meat and my eggs come from," Mama said, more to the roller towel than to Aunt Eunice. She seldom comes right back at her. And she never points out that Aunt Eunice eats her full quota of breasts and wishbones and starts every day she lives with two new eggs over easy. The give-and-take of their conversation went on, with Aunt Eunice giving and Mama taking. But I kept on looking out the window.

In that direction a mile or so is Mount Yeomans, our postal address, and nothing but a low rise out of flat land. There's a church spire at the crown, a grain elevator at the base, and rooftops in between. Neither a mountain nor a town, as my dad always says.

Beyond Mount Yeomans in the distance is the county seat, Dunthorpe. By day you can just make out the plumes of smoke from the industry. At night the lights wink and glow, spreading out, heading our way. Dad always says that when Dunthorpe gets as far as us, he'll subdivide and sell out. Then he and Mama will go down to Sun City, Arizona, and sit pretty.

And Mama gives him a look and says Dunthorpe never will grow that big, hoping she's right. Hoping she won't ever have to sit pretty down at Sun City with sand under her feet instead of hen grit.

I don't know how far Aunt Eunice's vision goes because I don't know where it begins. But Mama's vision stops at Mount Yeomans. It's all the town she needs. Mine goes farther. On that September day last fall when the chickens were dying before frying and the marigolds were in full flower, my mind was already stretched as far as Dunthorpe.

And though I'd spent my sophomore year at the high school there, I'd always tried to look a little beyond. Out past Dunthorpe to the level line of the horizon where I always had seen visions of my own.

A city where there were people forever dressed up in their party clothes and the ladies in long gowns. And little all-glass houses on the tops of skyscrapers where I danced in swirling skirts past snow-white grand pianos and across black marble floors to endless music. Where the garden-variety wren, Verna Henderson of R.F.D. Mount Yeomans was a dazzler of rare delight. I never quite knew where or what that city was. But I was sure it had to be a place that made Dunthorpe seem no bigger than Mount Yeomans, if as big.

I don't suppose dreams like that do you any harm, as long as you know they're dreams. In fact, I can't really see how a person could do without them.

It was the day before school took up again. One of those days when September might just as well be August. The air had no crispness about it, and the hedgerows were furry with dust. A shiftless day when everything's either over or not yet begun.

So I was about ready for school again and the 7 A.M. rendezvous down at the mailbox with the bus to Dunthorpe. My brother Hal had already gone back to college. Once he's gone, it's the end of summer for me. He always seems to take everything with him when he goes. There's too much room at the supper table without him. Even Aunt Eunice feels it.

But before Hal went back to Purdue, we had our little late-summer time together as usual. We never had to plan it. We'd always take off one early afternoon in the truck and head out to Persimmon Woods Reservoir.

It's the water supply for the county, a man-made lake in the middle of nowhere. You have to open a gate to get to it, and we know where there's a rowboat. Out in the dead center of the reservoir it's like floating on a mirror—clouds above and clouds below. We always took books, but we never did any reading. We'd talk a little, drift a lot.

I remember once when I was about eight and Hal was thirteen and we were out there. I don't know how it happened that he was rowing me around Persimmon that time. Up till then he hadn't taken any more notice of me than was absolutely necessary. And it was almost evening that time, so we didn't have any business to be out there in the first place. But I'll never forget it.

The sun was just down to the treeline. There was every color there is in the sky. The lake seemed on fire, with that silhouette of shoreline black as cinders all around. And so quiet you had to whisper.

Hal began telling me a story. I think it was meant to spook me, and it did a little. But it went beyond that. He said that back in the days when they flooded the land to make the reservoir there was a little town smack in the middle of it. One day the bulldozers just pushed their way in and all the people who lived there were told they had to get out.

This got me interested right away, so I asked him what the name of the town had been. He thought for a minute. Then he said it was Weavers Rest. (Now how do you suppose he came up with a name like that?)

Anyway, in the story all the people in the town had to scatter to the four winds. One day the water came in. A trickle down the gutters at first. Then rivers where the streets had been. Then only the second stories of the houses were left, with the curtains blowing out of the windows. And things floating by, like sofa cushions and the children's toys.

Finally nothing cleared the waterline but the church steeple with the weather vane on top. And pretty soon it stuck up like a solitary cattail in the middle of the lake. Then the water closed over that even. Hal made a little gurgling sound in his throat so I could hear exactly how the water sounded when it swallowed up the weather vane.

He waited so I could absorb all this. Then he said the boat we were in was just three feet above the church steeple. That if we dropped a hook and line we'd snag the weather vane sure as anything. I was gooseflesh and cockleburs all over to think we were floating that very minute over a ghost town, like ghosts ourselves. By then I'd clean forgotten that I didn't believe the story anyway.

But Hal wasn't finished. He said that sometimes on a very quiet evening, just around sundown, you could hear the bells in the church steeple chiming. Of course you had to listen with all your ears to hear bells tolling under water. And if there was any other noise around, like fish jumping or water lapping the boat, you wouldn't hear anything at all.

I remember my mouth was open, but I wasn't making a sound. It was quiet enough to hear the bells, quiet enough to hear anything. And I thought about how the currents of water really could drift through the belfry and ring the bells in a soft, watery way. And how fish might be swimming in and out where the stained glass windows had been and maybe an old crawdaddy on the pulpit.

It seemed so sad. And so beautiful. That little town, Weavers Rest, where nobody lived, like the castle in an aquarium. With the mossy bells gently ringing, making hardly any noise, and no one to call to prayer anyway. And there we were, Hal and I, hovering over it all while the lake turned silvery around us. Of course I cried. Because it was so weird and lonesome and beautiful. Because Hal had told it.

Every summer we'd go back. Hal very nearly made me cry again out there last summer. We were in the boat the day before he left to go back for his senior year. He was pulling on the oars and saying very little. I was in my bathing suit with the unfortunate hole in the seat that I can't wear anywhere but to the reservoir. Hal had his shirt off, but he was already as brown as he gets since he'd worked all summer in the field with Dad.

We got out to our place in the middle of the lake, right over the "steeple." And I knew the minute he brought the oars up that something was on his mind.

Just to prime the pump, I said, "Where do you suppose you'll be next year at this time? You'll be graduated by then."

And he said right back, "Oh, I suppose I'll be married or something."

Then he trained his eyes on me to see how I took this news. And I trained mine back on his and thought I saw nervousness. This information didn't come as any shock to me anyway. I knew he'd been up in his room writing letters every other night all summer, and that could only point to one thing. Mama sensed something in the wind too, but she was waiting to be told. What Dad knew was anybody's guess.

I figured if I started begging for details, he'd get quiet. So I just lolled there in the boat and let my hand slip down to the water.

"Maybe right after graduation," he said finally, "if I find a decent job and we can get settled into a place to live . . . and things work out."

It's funny how boys think they're the ones who make the plans, I thought but didn't say.

"What's she like?"

"Sherri? She's—different."

"In race, color, or creed?"

"No. Nothing like that. She's just different . . . from us." I waited. The boat drifted. It was quiet enough to hear church bells.

"She's a stewardess. You know, with an airline."

That rocked the boat a little. (HI! I'm Sherri, FLY ME!) That's different all right. Where'd he meet her?

"Where'd you meet her?"

"Oh, at kind of a party."

"But where?"

"At school. She has a friend who's in a sorority, and she was visiting, and they had a party I went to."

The thought of Hal at a party in a sorority house was

more than I could imagine. And I imagine very well for a farm girl. Now there's no question but that he's the best-looking boy in America and no doubt welcome everywhere. But I couldn't picture him at a sorority house where everything's pink and charming and crystal chandeliers, if that's what they're like. But then for me, as soon as Hal left the farm, he ceased to be.

"Well, when are you going to bring her home so we can have a look at her?" Right then I saw Hal's worst worry written all over his face. So I changed my tack. "I'll bet she's pretty, isn't she? They have to be."

"She's pretty all right."

"But different."

"Boy, is she different," Hal sighed. And then he started rowing for shore. "Don't say anything to anybody yet. I haven't gotten everything worked out," he said as we beached the boat.

It was only later that night when I was tucked up in bed that it really hit me. That things change. This had really been the last summer in lots of ways. Hal and I wouldn't be rowing out at Persimmon Woods again. It probably wouldn't ever be just the two of us again, even for one afternoon out of the year.

I knew Hal was grown up. To me he'd always been grown up. But I wished he wouldn't go hurrying off into the world before anything had happened to me. I'd just turned sixteen that summer and wanted something wonderful to happen—anything at all, but nothing much had.

So while I was trying to get to sleep, I decided to think about school and about being a junior in the fall and about the group of girls I know and things like that. But these thoughts didn't distract me any because pretty soon there were tears running out of the sides of my eyes, tears for Hal and maybe me, even though I'd decided it shouldn't be any crying matter.

chapter
two

The minute I'd heard about the group, I wanted to belong. I don't know now why I figured they owed me membership. But I never rested till they took me in. It's a wonder they did, and a bigger wonder that I cared.

I wasn't bused in to Dunthorpe until tenth grade because there's a grade school at Mount Yeomans for us "country children." It only runs up to eighth grade officially, but since the Dunthorpe high schools don't start till tenth grade, we have to horse around at the Mount Yeomans grade school an extra year. There were only three or four of us in a class there anyhow, so it doesn't make much difference.

By the time they've got us integrated with the town kids, we're all in sophomore year, and the groups are already pretty well set up. Believe me, you don't make much of an entrance onto that scene by climbing down out of a school bus carrying a lunch bucket.

But I had my wits about me. In a few days I was out of the dresses Mama and I had made me for town and into the dull denim and crumpled corduroy and army surplus everyone wears there. You should have seen the look on Dad's face the first day he saw me heading off to the bus in a bleached-out old Levi jacket of Hal's. "I wouldn't go to the barn lot in it," he said. "I got too much respect for the hogs." But he just shook his head and grinned.

Well, in Dunthorpe they did more than grin at me in the beginning. They laughed at the way my hair was until I pulled it down smooth and tucked it behind my ears the way they do. Listen, it took a while to get as plain as they like to look.

And they laughed at the way I talked till they got used to it. They even laughed at the lunch in my bucket. And when they tired of laughing, they got used to me and never realized I had to get used to them too. If I'd been a beauty, of course, the boys would have gotten used to me the first day. But then the girls never would have. So there you are.

At Dunthorpe Central High they've got a club for everything. Chess, Varsity Baton, Black Belt Karate, Debate, Young Americans for Immediate Social Change, Glee Club, Girls' Athletic Association, Yearbook, Friends of Kung Fu, Pep Club Cheerleaders, National Honor Society, Yoga, Camera Bug, Skeet Shooting, and I don't know what all. The only ones they don't have are Four-H and Future Farmers of America because of course they're much too citified for them.

twenty-four

It wasn't any of those I had my eye on. Not a club at all, but a bunch of town girls that ran around together. Nice girls and not snobbish when you get to know them. I don't know what possessed me, but the minute I identified them, I set my mind to belong. It seemed a whole lot better than spending three years like a Displaced Person, climbing on and off that everlasting bus.

I don't know what made me think I could get in with them, but I remember one time after school Mama and I were sitting at the kitchen table, and I was telling her about them. She heard me out, and then all she said was, "Don't get your feelings hurt." I saw right there she didn't figure they'd want me. I guess that decided the matter.

There's a lot to be said for just being present and not posing a threat to anybody. Pretty soon I was in with them, even if it was mostly just on school time at first. As groups go, they were all pleasant enough and broadminded if it didn't give them any trouble. Which is the way most people are, I guess. And to put it in a nutshell, I was their token yokel.

It didn't take me too long to work my way in. If it had, I might have lost interest. By the middle of last year we were all eating our lunch at the same table. They ate off trays. I ate out of my bucket.

In my own way I was as smart as two of them and smarter than the other two. And more practical than all four. Which is not the worst way of entering a group. But I learned from them all—things about town life. It was foreign territory to me, as foreign as mine was to them. They were bonehead ignorant about farm life until I undertook to educate them a little when the time was right. They'd been raised to believe the food grew on their dinner plates. And they never seemed to have stepped off sidewalks in their lives.

Until then, I'd almost never been inside a house in town. Bernice Ransom had the first gathering I was in on because it's her way to do the thoughtful thing before anybody else thinks about doing it. Her mother had been a Sinclair, which means something in Dunthorpe. And Bernice's dad owns the Kut-Rate Kornucopia supermarket.

Bernice was still in the hands of the orthodontist, so she had to speak through a wire hoop in her mouth. She's naive and nice and the closest thing the group has to a lady. The Ransoms live in the old Sinclair place, which looks like a farmhouse on a city street but is dressed up with shutters and lights in the lawn under the bushes. We eat very well at Bernice's. And her mother weighs in at two hundred pounds.

Then there's Merry-Beth ("Moon") Moody. Her mother keeps a loom in their living room. Her dad, who's a lawyer for the cornstarch works, has a pottery kiln in the basement. The Moody family subscribes to forty-two different magazines, and Moon wears smocks with Polish embroidery over Levi pants. In tenth-grade Social Problems class she wrote a paper on the subject of *vasectomy*, which was a thing I'd never even heard tell of before.

And there's Ludmilla Shaw, who's the only member of the group you can really get some conversation out of unless you want to hear Moon speak on vasectomies, social evils, Women's Rights, and migrant field hands. The Shaws live on the best street in town in an enormous, all-brick house with a crack in every window.

There's crabgrass and a dry fountain in the yard. The Shaws are said to be the craziest family in Dunthorpe, and though Ludmilla seems sane enough, it may be true. She has one brother at the state university and another one in the state hospital. She's planning to enter Vassar College at Poughkeepsie, New York. And she's in training for it by wearing woolen knee socks, tweeds, and her own very severe looks. If we'd let her, she'd be the leader of our group.

I've saved the star till last. She'd have been the undoing of a good many groups, I suppose. Because she's the dumbest, most beautiful girl that anyone ever heard of. Ten minutes worth of her company is the equal of ten hours. Yet a momentary glance from her empty eyes turns boys to beasts. Men too. You can just about see the hair sprouting on their palms.

Her name is Darlene Hoffmeister. It was Darlene who brought fame to our group this past year, if fame's the word for it. Whatever it was, it challenged all my visions of far-off glamour and enchantment.

It wasn't well-mannered Bernice. Or Moon with her social conscience. Or bossy Ludmilla's deranged family background. Or Verna, the lunchbucket peasant. It was

Darlene. It would be. And of all people in this world, I was the one who got caught up the most completely in Darlene's glory.

But long before I first knew her, Darlene must have been dynamite. I don't imagine she ever even went through an awkward age, physically speaking. She'd have been the kind to come out in beauty marks in place of pimples. If she hadn't been so simple that she needed leading around, we probably wouldn't have had anything to do with her. That and the fact that she was too sensational for competition.

There was poor old Bernice fighting for every breath behind all that hardware in her mouth. And Moon whose smocks concealed no figure at all. And Ludmilla who claimed her mind was on higher things. And me trying hard to pass for town and keep my hair tucked behind my ears. For a while back then I don't think Darlene knew what she had. She'd turn the boys on without aiming to, but they'd keep their distance from her. I guess she was food for their fantasies.

It was probably her mother who broke the news to her about her looks. Darlene is the product of a broken home. She often says so in just those words. And almost always to people who know it already. There's very little about Dunthorpe that people there don't already know.

When she gives her product-of-a-broken-home speech, I don't think she's looking for pity, which is a good thing because she wouldn't get any. I think it's just something interesting she knows about herself.

twenty-eight

Back when I was first going to their houses, it took all my thought to figure out how I could be with the group after school and even some evenings and still get home without the school bus. In a pinch my dad would drive in the ten miles, but he didn't like it.

At college vacation time when Hal was home, he'd drive in and pick me up. But he'd never come in the houses. Somebody's mother was always saying, "Have your brother in for a cup of coffee or something," but I'd make an excuse for him because I knew he wouldn't. He'd be in his work clothes or smelling like the barn, and so I couldn't get him out of the car. It was always a letdown to me because I wanted them to see my brother. He's as gorgeous as Darlene, and way smarter.

I'd come home and tell Mama everything about it. Mama always thinks town people live better than we do and know less. And some of the things I'd tell her she'd be surprised at.

When I'd been to Ludmilla's house, for example. In the Shaws' living room they have wonderful old wine-colored oriental rugs, but the only thing to sit on is furniture they've hauled in off the porch. Old wicker one-armed chairs and broken three-legged settees and the ceiling thick with cobwebs. And Ludmilla's mother drifting around the house looking like the Ghost of Christmas Yet to Come with the hem hanging out of her dress.

I played it way down though on the times I'd been to Darlene's house. She and her mother live in a split-level out in a suburb called Belvedere Hills. It's a nice place to live, with the houses all built around a stand of cottonwood trees. But every blessed thing in the Hoffmeisters' house is turquoise. Every wall in every room, and that counts the velveteen striped wallpaper in the powder room and the chenille cover on the toilet tank. I couldn't live with it.

Darlene is a natural blonde, of course, and her mother's an assisted redhead. So I guessed they figured that turquoise is the color that sets them both off. Mrs. Hoffmeister doesn't do anything. "I live on alimony and anticipation, darling," she once told me. And what was I supposed to make of that? I hadn't even asked her what she lived on, and wouldn't.

I got the shock of my early life at that house one time. We all came home with Darlene after school on the spur of the moment. Naturally, Darlene had lost her door key so she had to lean on the bell for a quarter of an hour before her mother let us in. She wasn't any too happy to see us either. She was hitching down her pants suit and running a hand through that red hair she dresses up high like a lion's mane. But she put on her social face and disappeared out into the turquoise kitchen to see if she could find us something to eat.

I got nominated to take all our coats and leave them on Darlene's bed. So I went on up with them, but those little halfway stairs in split-level houses are confusing. Upstairs, I turned the wrong way. Instead of going into Darlene's room, I walked straight into Mrs. Hoffmeister's.

thirty

And there in the bed was a man, sitting up and just as surprised to see me as I was to see him. And it was four o'clock in the afternoon too.

It scared me so bad I dropped all five coats on the floor. When I went down to pick them up, he went down under the sheet and stayed there. Not a word was exchanged, and I stumbled backwards out of the door and raced over to Darlene's room.

The first thought in my head was that Mr. Hoffmeister had come back home from wherever he'd run off to. But I didn't think that very long because the man in the bed couldn't have been more than twenty-five years old, if that. I only caught a glimpse of him, but I knew that much. He was naked as a jaybird too.

I never told, until last summer and then only to Hal when we were pushing the boat out at Persimmon Woods. He laughed so hard I thought he'd let the boat get away from us. But I never breathed a word of it otherwise, not even to Ludmilla, Bernice, and Moon, who'd all have been very interested.

By the end of tenth grade there'd been quite a little bit of socializing. But nobody had ever suggested coming out to the farm. It was always more convenient to go to somebody's house in town. Finally, I was a little put out that nobody seemed to give a thought to where I came from. Not even Ludmilla, who often had thoughts.

Of course it was up to me to do the inviting, but something held me back. I wanted them to see where we lived just in case they thought it was primitive (which is what I was sure they thought). But I was a little edgy somehow. I kept saying to myself they ought to come when the place is at its best—flowers in the garden and the oil on the lane not too fresh and Hal at home.

That was just procrastinating, though. I guess I'd spent so much time fitting in with them that bringing them out home was like undoing all the effort I'd put forth. It's peculiar what your mind gets up to at the age of fifteen. Any little thing can get out of proportion. In fact, I guess you've got to watch it all your life.

Then one day in June right out of a clear sky Mama said, "Don't you ever want to have the girls out? Seems like you owe them." I think she'd been procrastinating too, though she's not one to put off paying people back. She might have been holding off, thinking I was ashamed of home or something. She never said anything, but I knew her eye was on me, watching to see if I was getting so citified that I wouldn't be fit to live with.

So the great day came almost before I knew it. I'd been ready to jump in with both feet and make all the plans, though I don't know what plans I'd have made. But that isn't Mama's way. If people are coming, she's going to have things the way that seems right to her.

It was at the end of finals week. We had a half day off from school. The group rode out right after noon with me on the school bus. Those four getting on the bus with their bathing suits in canvas bags were a study. They looked at the kids who rode regularly as if they'd never laid eyes on them before, which in a way may have been the truth.

Bernice was the only one in a skirt. Ludmilla was wearing an old pair of jodhpurs and a workshirt. Moon wore one of her smocks but without the Levi pants underneath. She had her hair jerked up under a red bandanna. And she spent the trip reading a paperback called *Sowing the Seeds of Sorrow: A Study in the Exploitation of Farm Labor.* Darlene was wearing . . . I can't remember what. With her it's often hard to recall. Because of that luscious body, all curves going the right directions, and that face as fresh as all the lilies of the field. And those eyes like two marbles scooped out on the underside.

"Where will we swim? Is there a pool?" Ludmilla wanted to know.

"You'll see," I said.

"No, not a pool," Bernice said. "There'll be a pond where the cattle go down to drink at evening."

"You'll see."

Moon was silent throughout, her eyes boring holes into *Sowing the Seeds of Sorrow,* and her head nodding in silent outrage. Darlene wasn't her usual rattling self either. She'd been unusually quiet for several days, not that anybody minded.

Mrs. Bergschneider from Mount Yeomans drives the bus. When she pulled up to our mailbox and cranked the door open, I had to shoo the group off like a mother hen. They couldn't see the house from there.

"It must be an *estate!*" Bernice said, looking up the

lane. Both sides of it are planted in corn, and there are oak trees up by the house to screen it from the road. Those four nearly fractured their ankles walking as far as the yard. But they chattered on about how fresh the air was till you'd have thought they were all from Chicago.

Just as we came up on the porch, Aunt Eunice opened the screen door, and of course they all took her for my mother. I hadn't thought to mention Aunt Eunice. She gave their clothes a look, I can tell you. But Mama came right out behind her and made them welcome.

We went upstairs to change into bathing suits. On the way I saw Mama had put out bowls of garden flowers on every flat surface. There was even a little nosegay of button daisies on the back of the bathroom sink. When they saw how big the bathroom was, they all had to start changing clothes in there at once. They'd never seen a bathroom made out of a bedroom before. And all the shrieking and whooping we did getting changed was enough to wake the dead.

Then we trooped down the stairs in our beach attire and ragged tennis shoes and went out the side door. When we got out on the porch, I heard Aunt Eunice say from inside, "Well if that wasn't a sight to sour milk!"

I led them down across the lot and along by the implement shed to where we could cut across the pasture. We weren't going out to the reservoir. That was a place I hadn't shared but with one person. Instead, we went to the branch, which isn't any more than three feet deep at the best of times and hardly any wider. They didn't even recognize it as water until they were right up to it.

But good old Bernice took off her shoes, lined them up, and waded in, with Ludmilla not far behind. Moon spread her towel and stretched out to continue with her reading, and Darlene posed on the bank like a page from a calendar.

Then all at once Bernice let out a scream that must have set her wire hoop vibrating. She pointed to the middle of the creek. Then her feet went out from under her, and she was flat on her back in the branch. Ludmilla caught a gallon of brown water right in the face. Bernice flailed around and tried backpedaling her feet to get to the bank. And when she got up on it, she slipped in the mud and fell right down on her back again, this time in the weeds. "Oh look right there on that rock!" she said before she could get up.

Sure enough, there was an old mud turtle as still as the stone he was on. "Is it *poisonous?*" Bernice wailed. And that was as near as she got to water the rest of the afternoon. Later on, I saw the tail of a blue racer flip through the undergrowth on the far side of the branch, but I didn't let on. What town eyes don't see doesn't worry them.

When the sun got over in the west, we started back to the house, with all concerned feeling pretty satisfied that they had good starts on their tans. Before we were up to the yard, I was looking to see if Mama had set up the folding picnic tables, but they weren't in sight.

It was still early, so we went down to the barn lot. Hal, who'd just come home from Purdue, was out in the field somewhere, but Dad was down there, draining the oil out of the tractor. He looked kind of amused to see us all, but he swept off his cap when I made the introductions.

Right away, Ludmilla said to him, "Mr. Henderson, do you milk cows?"

Dad said, no, he let the calves do that. She looked a little puzzled, but let that pass. Moon didn't say anything, but she kept eyeing Dad to see if maybe he had a dozen or so migrant workers chained up back of the barn.

We drifted over to the hen house then, and Dad followed along behind for fear he'd miss something. I made them go right inside, though they'd have been happy enough to let it pass with a quick look.

I thought it was the time to tell them that I gather eggs in there every morning of the year before I set off for the bus. Which is *long* before they're out of bed. Well, the hen house smells like hen houses do, and there were four wrinkled up noses in there.

Suddenly Darlene broke the silence and said in a high squeak, "Oh, yuch—this place is just slick with . . . with—waddaya call it?—chickenshit!"

On that we left, but I discovered Dad behind the door. His hand was up over his eyes, and it was wet with tears. I took them back up to the house, leaving Dad behind the hen house door, slowly doubling up.

chapter
three

I got cleaned up and changed before the rest of them and went downstairs to see if I could help Mama. When I walked through the dining-room door on the way to the kitchen, my eyes started out of my head. The room looked like every holiday on the calendar with somebody's wedding feast added for good measure.

The table had the extra leaves and the cutwork company tablecloth. There were candles, yellow ones, in the glass holders. Between them in a straw basket was a centerpiece. A combination of black-eyed Susans and Queen Anne's lace surrounded by strawberry leaves. Sticking up from this were the snapped-off heads from stalks of wheat.

The good dishes were out, of course. Grandma Henderson's Havilland with the wispy gold rims and the faded little antique rosebuds. All the cut glass was there too, filled with bread-and-butter pickles, celery stuffed with cream cheese and chives, and radish rosettes. There was a Jello salad like a Christmas wreath, decorated with pineapple rings and those bright green, minty cherries.

The table's bare spots were where the platters of fried chicken would go, and the pocketbook rolls. I could smell them in the oven that minute, rising up golden and yeasty.

I stood there a moment and ruminated. I thought about how there's never anything in Moon Moody's refrigerator whenever we go to raid it. And how Ludmilla's mother will bring out iced tea in five unmatching jam jars. And of the mountain of peanut butter and Ritz crackers and cocktail onions we'd eaten at Darlene Hoffmeister's. And while there's a variety at Bernice's house, it's all straight from the boxes and cans of the Kut-Rate Kornucopia supermarket.

While I was having these thoughts, Mama came in from the kitchen. She had on a crisp new cotton dress and a fancy, for-show-only apron. In her hands was a big bowl of potato salad with hard-boiled eggs sliced over the top. She stopped when she saw me there. Her gaze fluttered over at the table and then met mine. And she looked—shy.

"Oh, Mama," I said, and then I had to swallow hard. I had an impulse to go over and put my arms around her. After it's too late, I always wish I'd follow impulses like that. But at least I got something said, "Oh, Mama, it's perfect."

Somewhere from the kitchen came Aunt Eunice's

muffled voice, talking to itself, "I hope it'll be appreciated."

Dad and Hal came in all slicked up from the room behind the kitchen where they do their changing and washing up. Dad had the line across his forehead, white above and red below, that his cap makes. And Hal had his dark blond hair pretty well under control though longer than Dad thinks is right. They both looked at the table in wonderment, but didn't say anything. Mama got very busy all of a sudden and said, "You'd better get those girls down here because it's all as ready as it's going to be."

I don't know what went over bigger with the girls that night—the fried chicken or Hal. There was such a pile of bones on every plate that you couldn't see the rosebuds on the china. Even Bernice managed to nibble her share.

"I'd go bucktoothed all my days before I'd wear a thing like that in my mouth," Mama said later. "It's an instrument of torture." Moon and Darlene snapped four wishbones between them. Darlene got the long, wish-come-true part every time.

I couldn't help but think how it would curb their appetites to see how Mama wrings the necks off those chickens.

To make conversation, Ludmilla asked Dad if the hogs fed off table scraps. He said no, they eat hog concentrate, which costs a fortune and is continually on the rise. Moon looked up pretty sharp at this as if she was going to frame a question about the feed-hog profit margin. But apparently *Sowing the Seeds of Sorrow* hadn't given her any background on that.

They ate up everything in sight and told Mama a hundred times how good it all was. But whenever I happened to notice, one or the other of them was casting a long look at Hal. He regarded them in return the way a college junior will regard a bunch of fifteen-year-old girls, only Hal was polite. I did catch him staring at Darlene, though, and more than once.

He told me later it looked to him like they all had possibilities of one kind or another. Except maybe for Moon, who was trying too hard. Generally speaking, I didn't think that was far from the truth.

Mama brought in a big layer cake with caramel icing and a thick sprinkling of chopped walnuts on top. She started to sit down. Then she bobbed up again and brought out a big bowl of fresh strawberries, frosted with powdered sugar.

We were all ready to tear into this when lights flashed out in the lane. A car pulled up into the loose gravel by the front gate. Dad got up and turned on the pole light, which set the dogs barking. We could hear high heels pecking up the walk. Mama surveyed the cake to see if it would stretch to another piece, and Dad went out to the hall. I could hear him swinging open the screen door and say, "Why yes, you've got the right place. Step right in."

There was a further murmur of voices, and then into

the dining room stepped Mrs. Hoffmeister, looking like a Hollywood star. Hal stumbled to his feet, looked at her, then glanced at Darlene. Then back at Mrs. Hoffmeister. She knew how to make an entrance. There was a short pause while we absorbed her white linen dress and the long turquoise scarf caught up on her shoulder by a big gold pin in the shape of a lion's head. Her hair was redder than ever, each fiery strand in place.

Then all at the same time there was a crossfire of voices. I said, "Mama, this is Mrs. Hoffmeister."

She said, "I hope you'll forgive me for intruding, Mrs. Henderson."

And Mama said, "Oh take a chair please. There's plenty to eat." Through all this, Darlene looked on dully as if she'd never set eyes on the woman before.

When it came Hal's turn to be introduced, Mrs. Hoffmeister gave him a melting look like she was preparing to lead him down a garden path somewhere. Dad slipped a chair in under her. Before she knew where she was, she had a plate of layer cake and a dish of strawberries before her.

She's a smooth woman, that Mrs. Hoffmeister, when the circumstances call for it. She exclaimed over how pretty the table looked. Then she said, "And which one of you ladies is responsible for this cake? Which drew in both Aunt Eunice and Mama.

Aunt Eunice, as bright and friendly as you please, said, "I do the boiled caramel icing, and Edith, she does the baking itself."

"The texture is *absolutely superb,*" Mrs. Hoffmeister said, and you couldn't tell whether she meant the icing or the cake. Only then did she look across the table and say, "Hi, Darlene honey, how are you?"

"Hello, Mother," Darlene said, "what are you doing here?" It was the question in all our minds.

"Well, baby, I just had to come out, and I hope nobody minds my crashing the party"—heads shook no all around the table—"but I just got some news over the phone this evening that was *absolutely* too good to keep. I simply couldn't wait for you to come home, Darlene sweetie. I was just *bouncing* with it!" By then she had us all in the palm of her hand, possibly even Darlene who was watching her through narrow lids.

"You remember, honey, how I sent in those photographs of you to the beauty contest—" Mrs. Hoffmeister said, her eyes sweeping around to fill us in before returning to Darlene, "the contest that Midstates Hybrid Seed Corn Company in Bloomington is holding? You know the Midstates Hybrid Seed Corn Company, I expect, Mr. Henderson," she said, suddenly turning toward Dad.

"I know it well," he said.

"Yes, of course," she said to him and the rest of us, leaving Darlene out, "I heard they were holding a contest and I sent in some studio photos of Darlene and—she won!"

"Well I never," said Mama.

"Neither did I," said Aunt Eunice.

"So this means," Ludmilla said, "that Darlene—"

"Is MISS HYBRID SEED CORN!" Mrs. Hoffmeister finished. "There's a small cash prize, and Darlene will be featured in all the Midstates Hybrid Seed Corn Company advertising—billboards and television and—" Suddenly Mrs. Hoffmeister shifted down, and just in time. She lowered her voice and riveted Mama and Aunt Eunice again, "Of course, you realize that had it involved Darlene putting on a bathing suit and parading around scantily attired on a stage in front of a lot of men judges, I couldn't have allowed it, and I know you'd be the same."

Mama nodded, but belatedly.

"And," she went on, "I wouldn't want to think that anything like this would go to Darlene's head."

"Oh I don't think it'll go to her head," Ludmilla said, but so innocently that she got away with it.

"I think it's just great," said Bernice. "Congratulations, Darlene. I'm positive you were the prettiest contestant, and you deserve it."

Darlene had been the quiet eye of the storm. But she looked past her mother to Bernice and said, "Thank you. It's a great honor."

For some reason it was the oddest thing I'd ever heard Darlene say. For a start, it was very dignified. She always had looked a lot older than she was, and suddenly she sounded even older than she looked. It was an all-new Darlene, like she was just being hatched out. Newborn and triumphant. It quieted the room down, and somehow it seemed to be directed against her mother.

But it was Moon who found her tongue first. "Exploitative," she said. Hal snorted once but straightened his face.

"I beg your pardon, dear?" said Mrs. Hoffmeister and glittered at her.

"It's *exploitative*," Moon repeated. "Exploitative of the female body to pander to chauvinistic male lust in the name of crass commercialism." At that, Darlene lapsed into her old self, not having understood a single syllable.

It gave Mrs. Hoffmeister her finest moment though. She looked directly at Moon, and her eyes spoke an entire sentence that everyone seemed to be able to hear. And the sentence was *Don't worry, my dear; it will never happen to you.* Moon crumpled.

All the girls rode back to town with Mrs. Hoffmeister. After they were gone, we Hendersons sat around the dining-room table, watching the candles burn down. I was feeling rosy inside about the whole day. Even Mrs. Hoffmeister's bombshell had added something, though it had tended to break up the party. A touch of high drama to top things off.

Hal and Dad were off to one side chuckling about how Darlene had spent the whole afternoon surrounded by hybrid seed corn and was none the wiser, which of course had nothing to do with anything.

"I'm sure I don't know if it's right," Aunt Eunice said. "A girl not yet sixteen years old plastered up on sign posts."

forty-four

"She really is a right pretty girl," Mama said.

"Pretty is as pretty does," said Aunt Eunice.

"You could see how proud of her Mrs. Hoffmeister is," Mama said.

"If that woman's hair is her own," Aunt Eunice said, "I'm Chinese."

That night was the beginning. Something historic had blossomed right there in our dining room. It was to go on flowering too. The publicity began at once with a front-page article in the *Dunthorpe Morning Call*. There was a picture of Darlene and her mother grouped tastefully in their living room. Over it, the headline read:

LOCAL LOVELY NAMED CORN QUEEN

For the rest of the summer and well beyond you couldn't go anywhere without coming across Darlene's picture, sometimes twenty feet high. There was even a poster stuck up in the grain office at Mount Yeomans showing Darlene smiling over her shoulder at a field of corn. Both she and the corn were larger than life and looking unusually ripe.

Midstates Hybrid Seed Corn Company wanted their money's worth. Darlene's ravishing face and exploited figure went on to promote such Midstates products as chicken feed, hog mash, dog chow, sheep-dip, rodent killer, and a nutriment guaranteed to turn runts into porkers overnight.

And even this was only a beginning.

chapter
four

In the summer the group disintegrated
temporarily. Moon and her mother went off to Okaw
Valley State College to take a summer school course
called Consciousness-raising and Community Advocacy.
Her dad stayed home and practiced law for the starch
works. According to Moon, he was into yoga and organic
vegetables, which meant he stood on his head and kept
a garden. Label it new, and that family's all over it.

Bernice volunteered her time with the Dunthorpe
Recreation Department's summer playground program
for little kids. Ludmilla went with her family up to their
summer place at Rhinelander, Wisconsin, where they
always go.

A letter came from Ludmilla, the only one I got from
anybody all summer. It sounded just like her. She said
they spent their days up there with her dad in a boat
fishing without bait and her mother sitting on the pier,

talking to the water. She herself was improving her chances for admission to Vassar College by rereading *Silas Marner* and Jacqueline Susanne. I didn't hear anything from Darlene, but, as I said, you couldn't get far from her face.

It's funny how remote Dunthorpe becomes in the summer. Even Mount Yeomans fades into the distance and shimmers there like a mirage. The early morning sun bounces off the sheet-metal siding on the grain elevator. From my window I can look right down the bean rows while I'm dressing. Every day the summer squash vine creeps a little farther along the woven-wire fence, turning its big three-toed leaves up to the hot light.

On an especially stifling morning you can smell the onions down in the loose black soil. And all the world there is seems to stop at the end of our property line.

Mama keeps me busy. We start in June with the strawberries for jam, which we put up by the quart jar. Then we work on through the grapes and peaches. How some people live out their entire lives and never know the smell of sugared fruit simmering on the top of a stove I don't understand. Summer's a busy time, lonesome and cozy. I can settle back to being who I am and nothing else.

Very little happened in the early part of last summer except that Bess, the barn cat, had four kittens. I named them Bernice, Moon, Ludmilla, and Darlene, regardless of whatever sex they might turn out to be. One of them disappeared without so much as a telltale tuft. And long before it was weaned. It was either Moon or Bernice, I think. I decided not to try to think what happened to it. The loss didn't concern Bess any. In my darker moments I always have thought she was a bit of a kitten cannibal anyway.

There was something more important nagging at my mind though—about Hal. And this was before we went out to Persimmon Woods and he told me what little he had about Sherri and getting married. He'd started out at Purdue in a premed course. I can remember back in his freshman year when he and Dad had talked about his major. Dad hadn't encouraged him to take up agriculture. The future of farming seemed too uncertain, though it hurt him not to be able to urge Hal to come back so they could farm together.

"It's been a good living for us," Dad had said, "but I don't know if it'll support two families."

I think, though, that Hal had always had his heart set on doctoring—people medicine, I mean, not veterinary. But it didn't mean too much to me at the time—that major business. The whole idea of what went on at college was vague in my mind—in Mama's too.

But lately Hal never mentioned going on to medical school. And if he and Dad had held any conversations on the subject, I never heard them. Seemed like Hal was keeping his own counsel on the subject.

Every summer we decide we're definitely not going to the state fair. Hal and I say we've outgrown it. When he was still at the Mount Yeomans grade school, he'd had a Future Farmers heifer project. He and that heifer went off to the fair, and he slept in the pen with it for a week. He curried it like a show pony, showed it, and won third. The ribbon hangs on his bedroom wall to this moment. Those were the great days, we always say, and they can't be repeated.

Dad says the fair always falls right at the only time of year he has to mend the fences. Mama maintains she's seen enough prize-winning quilts and two-headed pullets to last her forever. And Aunt Eunice claims there's nothing to it but the biggest crowd of people with B.O. she ever saw.

And on an August morning every year, we're off to the fair and as early in the day as possible. Last summer was just like all the others before it. The chores were finished and breakfast over an hour ahead of time. We were all assembled in the kitchen and straining at the bit. All of us except Aunt Eunice.

She came down her stairway and looked around at us with astonishment all over her face. Then it seemed to come to her why we were all standing there, with Hal flipping the car keys in his hand.

"Oh, you all go on ahead without me," she said. "I won't go."

"Now, Eunice," Dad said, "There isn't any reason for you to stay behind."

"You can't just turn your back on property these days," she said, looking grim. "Anything could happen.

Besides, it doesn't make any difference to me whether I go or stay. Don't give me any thought."

Mama stood with her pocketbook planted under her arm waiting them out. She could see as plain as day that Aunt Eunice had on a fresh dress and a new starched hanky sticking up out of her bosom. And hose on. All she had to do was reach behind her on the stairway and pick up her purse and her sun hat. Then she'd be as ready as the rest of us.

So we were off, Aunt Eunice included, with no more than the usual delay. As soon as we got near the fairgrounds, it was like it always is. The creeping line of cars and open-bed trucks, full of down-home-type merrymakers. The little boys stand out by the curbs, waving the traffic in to park in the yards, all day for a dollar. Then in the distance that whine from the motorcycles on the race track and the jumpy music that runs up your back. Who'd miss it?

We separated at the car with elaborate plans for meeting up again. Dad and Hal went off to look at the machinery displays. I planned to walk Mama as far as the Centennial Building to see the gladiola show, and Aunt Eunice wanted to go that way too on her way to the Ideal Home Exhibit and the pastry judging. Aunt Eunice had quite a number of stops to make on her program.

"Every one of those hot dogs is poisoned meat," she remarked as we went past the Pronto Pup Terrace Cafe. "And would you just take a whiff of the grease they fry their potatos in? I'd bury it behind the cob house." It was a wonderful smell, mingled with spun-sugar candy and horse and whatever else there is that makes the fair smell like an unsanitary version of heaven.

We were fighting the crowds on that stretch of walk-way between the 4-H auditorium and the swine pavilion when I stopped dead. There coming toward us through the masses of farm women in print dresses was Mrs. Hoffmeister. She was striding along in a beige crepe pants suit and high heels, with a turquoise sash around her waist and sunglasses pushed up on the top of her red head.

Mama said, "Could that be—"

"It sure is," I said.

"Who?" said Aunt Eunice, "Where?"

She caught sight of us and came right over with her arms out. "*What* a heavenly surprise!" she said, "*What* an extraordinary coincidence!" Before we knew it, she had hold of all three of us somehow and was shepherding us into the 4-H auditorium right past a big sign that read

FESTIVAL OF BEAUTY QUEENS FASHION SPECTACULAR
SEE THE LOVELIEST GIRLS IN THE MIDWEST MODELING
THE LATEST SUMMER, TRANSITIONAL, AND FALL FASHIONS
BIG DESIGNER LABELS SELECTED FROM LEADING STORES
COMPLIMENTARY FLORIDA ORANGE JUICE   DOOR PRIZES
10 A.M. CURTAIN TIME
free admission

"You'll be my guests, of course," Mrs. Hoffmeister said.

The hall was filling up fast as free events will. But

down we went to the front where there was a roped-off section for the families of the Loveliest Girls in the Midwest. I don't think any of us got a word said except for Mrs. Hoffmeister who never stopped talking as we settled into our folding chairs. "Naturally you can imagine how *thrilled* Darlene was to take part in a statewide fashion show. I've had her parading up and down the house for a month with a book on her head. You know I think a thing like this is so good for the posture.

"Don't you feel, Mrs. Henderson, that all these experiences build poise and self-confidence?"

Mama thought that probably they did. On the other side of me Aunt Eunice said in that voice that carries, "How long do you figure this will go on?" Then somebody planted a Dixie cup of orange juice in her hand, and she settled back, keeping one hand on her pocketbook.

The loudspeaker was blaring out songs: "You Came Out of a Dream" and "A Pretty Girl is like a Melody." But through the music I could hear snatches of Mrs. Hoffmeister's conversation, ". . . so gratifying that Darlene is having these opportunities . . . basically really very shy . . . afraid even a little—backward—in certain . . . terribly important to have wholesome friends like your daughter. . . ."

Mama was keeping her dignity. I could feel it in her shoulder brushing mine. But she was beginning to eat out of Mrs. Hoffmeister's hand a bit, so to speak. It's really about the only way to deal with her.

The curtain went up, and a man in a white coat came out to a microphone. He had a lot of jokes and observations that were meant to warm up the audience, but missed the mark every time. When he got through, Mrs. Hoffmeister, sounding righteous, said to Mama, "I found some of that in rather questionable taste."

"You and me both," said Aunt Eunice, across Mama and me. But then a lady in a hat took over the microphone and said she was something called a fashion coordinator for one of the big Peoria stores. She explained about how all the girls modeling the clothes were beauty contest winners of one kind or another: Miss Cherry Blossom of Pinckney County, Miss Fire-Rite Spark Plug, Miss Public Services of Rock Island–Davenport, Miss Masonic Lodge, and so on, including of course Miss Hybrid Seed Corn. She told us how each girl would not only show off the clothes but make a "fashion commentary."

In a way it was exciting—certainly better than a gladiola show. And I was kind of rooting for Darlene, hoping she'd do her best. It wasn't a question of feeling jealous. I'm about 90 percent sure I didn't want to be up there on the stage myself. And no matter what the reward, I wouldn't want my mother pushing me like Darlene's was pushing her.

They started coming out, one at a time. They minced along and twirled and pirouetted and made their commentaries. It was Miss Chicago Lake Front who got all the daring numbers, slit up the side and no back. They had

Darlene pegged as the healthy, girl-next-door type, probably because of the seed corn ads.

But when she first walked onto the stage, I didn't recognize her. They had her made up, but that wasn't the main thing. She walked more like a real model than the rest of them. She nearly floated. And when she got up to the microphone, I didn't recognize her voice. How hard she must have worked to get that speech memorized, but it was the sound of her voice that was the best. A little stiff and singsongy, but very . . . developed. I remembered that night at our house when she'd thanked Bernice for congratulating her.

"This three-piece ensemble by Bettina Juniors, Limited, is equally at home on the campus or in the executive suite. . . ." Her eyes looked a little glassy as she stared out over the audience. But you could tell that almost everybody thought she was good. The women with their cardboard sun hats and funeral parlor fans murmured and smiled at her. But she didn't smile back. She was remembering her lines: ". . . in a synthetic blend fiber, while the jacket is an amusing variation on the classic blazer motif. . . ."

She opened up her jacket to show us the patterned lining and the little mustard-yellow waistcoat. Then she twirled around to show us the gored skirt and started back toward the wings. She didn't wiggle her bottom like Miss Chicago Lake Front. And she didn't wobble and fall off her heels the way Miss Veterans of Foreign Wars did. She was perfect. And she looked exactly like what she wasn't—a sophisticated, intelligent twenty-year-old girl.

"She did real well," Mama told Mrs. Hoffmeister.

"Oh do you think so? I do value your judgment, Mrs. Henderson." Just before it was over Mrs. Hoffmeister had to slip away to meet Darlene for a press party being held for the models. She whispered across to me how sorry she was that Darlene and I couldn't get together since Darlene had never been to the fair before, but I'd understand how every minute of their time was spoken for. She swept away then and floated down the aisle toward the stage.

Aunt Eunice was ready to slip off in the other direction, but we decided to sit it out through the door prizes. They gave away a hair dryer in a carrying case I wouldn't have minded having and a lady's electric shaver. Then they brought out an enormous box covered in blue velvet.

Inside it was full of Miss Misty brand perfumes and colognes—atomizers, purse flagons, sachets, bath oils, toilet water, eye shadow, a lipstick for every day in the week, and I don't know what all, nestled into ice-blue satin. The man in the white coat could hardly hold it. He dived into the bowl and pulled out seat number twenty-four.

Everybody shifted around to check the numbers on the backs of their chairs. But nobody rose up to claim the prize. The man in the white coat fiddled around, waiting for somebody to leap up screaming.

Finally, Mama gave a little jump and leaned over to me, "I'm in number twenty-two, and you're twenty-three, Verna. That puts Aunt Eunice in twenty-four."

I poked her, but she was just sitting there staring straight ahead, waiting with the rest of us. "That's you, Eunice," Mama hissed.

"What?" Aunt Eunice hitched around and looked at her chair number. "Oh my stars, I can't go up there on that stage!" "Hurry on," Mama said, "before he draws another number."

"Oh be quiet, Edith," Aunt Eunice said, "I could just *die*."

A great big woman behind us solved the whole problem by starting up and hollering out, "There she sets right there in front of me. There's the number twenty-four!"

Aunt Eunice whipped around and gave the big woman the look that kills. If they'd had a spotlight, they'd have turned it on her. As it was, the man on the stage pointed right at her and said, "There's the lucky little lady, and she's just too doggone excited to move!"

At that, Aunt Eunice moved. She got up, edged across our row, and headed down the aisle, a perfect sleepwalker. She managed to get up the steps, and while she crossed to center stage, the auditorium was so quiet we could all listen to her shoes squeak.

The man was tired of waiting on her, so he began before she was up close. "On behalf of the midwestern distributors of Miss Misty quality cosmetics of London,

England, and Paris, France, it's my profound pleasure to present you with the Empress Collection of Miss Misty beauty products for the beautiful woman, what's your name, honey?"

Aunt Eunice stared at him through her bifocals with her jaw down. She worked her mouth a moment and mumbled something.

"Folks, the lucky lady is Mrs. Eunice Henderson!"

"Miss," Aunt Eunice said in a voice the microphone picked up.

"Miss," said the man. "And how about you telling the folks where you come from, Miss Henderson."

Something came over Aunt Eunice then. She continued to look like she wanted to cut and run. But instead she turned slowly toward the audience and took one little step between the man and the microphone.

She reached for it. Her eyeglasses looked like two moons. She smiled a little bit which was an event in itself. Then she cleared her throat. "I'm from out in the country very near to Mount Yeomans. That's Black Hawk County over in the eastern part of the state. I'm here today with my sister-in-law and my niece who are out there somewhere. And of course the men came too, but they're over looking at the machinery. We're just seeing the fair today, we come every year and wouldn't miss it and thanks very much to all."

While Aunt Eunice was delivering this sermon, her voice got steadily stronger until the loudspeakers were whistling. The man behind her was trying to reach around to get his microphone back. But then she took her prize in both hands and marched off the stage to a round of applause. To tell you the truth, she wiggled her bottom just the slightest bit. The great big woman behind us clapped the loudest. And before Aunt Eunice got back to us, Mama had her handkerchief stuffed in her mouth and was ready to strangle on it.

Right then I started to consider what comes over people when the glare of publicity is upon them. Something does. Darlene was one thing, but Aunt Eunice would make anybody wonder.

It took us a while to get out of the auditorium since Aunt Eunice was a celebrity for a few minutes. People kept coming up to her to tell her how lucky she was. Aunt Eunice smiled and nodded and would have waved her hand at them like the queen of England if she hadn't been clutching her prize and her purse.

"We'd better nip on back to the car with that . . . box," Mama said.

"Oh no," Aunt Eunice said. "Let's not bother and waste the time. It isn't heavy." She was trying to park it up under one arm, but that wouldn't work. So she ended up with it in both hands and her purse perched on top. The Empress Collection of Miss Misty must have weighed fifteen pounds, and the box was an awkward heart shape at that. But she sailed off with it, and the crowd made way for her.

"We couldn't pry it off her with a crowbar," Mama murmured to me.

"What's that, Edith?" Aunt Eunice said. "Speak up."

The Women's Exchange Buffeteria is the only fair-grounds place where Aunt Eunice will eat. We met Hal and Dad outside it for lunch. Just to plague us, they were both wearing giveaway plastic farmers' caps, with "International Harvester" in big letters above the bills.

"Oh take those things off and stick them in a trash barrel," Mama said. "They're awful."

"Well I should think they are," said Aunt Eunice. To plague her specifically, neither Hal nor Dad asked how she came to be toting a heart-shaped velvet box three feet across. But during lunch we got all that told and about seeing Darlene in the Fashion Spectacular. Not that Dad or Hal took any more than a passing interest.

After lunch, we tend to take the fair at a dead run. The time seems to get away from us. Hal said, "Well, I guess Verna'll be wanting me to give her a ride on the merry-go-round."

That's an old battle cry between us. If there was a time when we actually did ride the merry-go-round, I can't remember it. As far back as I know, we've gone down to the carnival and picked out the meanest, scariest ride we can find. And that's the one we go on, Hal testing my courage and me proving it. We were about over all that kind of childishness by last summer. Almost, but not entirely.

So off we headed to Happy Hollow by ourselves, not quite hand-in-hand, but close. Two little kids again with ten cents to spend.

Happy Hollow is a dip in the fairgrounds over on a corner plot. Big, quiet-looking elm trees screen it from the more serious parts of the fair. Through the leaves you see the colored lights first: neon tubes revolving over the dodgem cars and the old-time blinking bulbs on the kiddie rides. And the sounds: the steam-organ music, the rumble of the tilt-a-whirl, the barkers urging everybody in to the bingo and the Hell-Drivers' Upside-Down Motorcycle Hippodrome.

The whole place crawls with people carrying balloons on sticks and sound asleep babies. The sawdust works into your shoes, and there's always a girly show the sheriff has shut down on the first day. To put the whole atmosphere in a sentence—Aunt Eunice won't go near the place.

"Well now, let's see," Hal said as we turned into the midway past the freak show, "we don't want to pick anything too scary on account of your nervous stomach, Verna."

"Don't worry about my stomach any. It'll go anywhere yours will."

"But will it come back?"

"Hmmm."

"I don't suppose there's any point to considering the roller coaster. It's just a bitty little thing. Not up in our class."

"Kid stuff," I said, not especially wanting to look up at the cars full of shrieking people mounting the top hill. We strolled on past the Caterpillar Underground Railway, The Tossing Teacups, the Astro-Rockets, and the Nickel Throw stand where you pitch for crockery.

"Not much of a carnival this year," Hal said, as he always does. He was only playing for time. By then we both knew the ride for us. It was at the end of the midway—the double Ferris wheel. Two Ferris wheels, in fact, one on top of the other and then exchanging positions. It looked rickety to me, but inevitable. After a short, tense wait, we were in the double seat. The safety bar banged shut between me and any idea of escape.

We swept up backwards and level with the treetops. Not bad, of course. But above us was another wheel whose passengers were revolving high above earth, trees, fair. I dreaded the moment.

"Do your eyes happen to be shut?" Hal asked.

"If yours were open, you'd know." I adjusted to the low level up over and down again. Coaxing one hand off the safety bar, I drew it into my lap. It lay there, fingers up like a softshell crab.

Then the whole wheel began making a shuddering swing. The wheels were changing places, and we were orbiting up and up over everything.

The softshell crab in my lap yearned to be a tarantula scrambling for a purchase on the safety bar. It seemed like we were taking off in an open-air jet plane, though at that time I knew nothing of a jet plane's ways.

We revolved on high. That leap for the sky had taken the wind out of Hal too. To prove it hadn't, he manufactured some small talk.

"So you saw Darlene strutting her stuff this morning."

"Yep."

"Looking good, was she?"

"Better than ever."

"Good for you."

"For me? It didn't have anything to do with me."

"Yes it did. Lots of girls—most girls—would be jealous and fixing to scratch her eyes out for getting too big for her britches."

I passed up a choice comment I could have made about Darlene's britches.

"And I'll tell you another thing," Hal said. "You're better than she is or ever will be." I was beginning to like this ride.

"Well, I have more sense than she does, but then most everybody does."

"You don't have to tell me that. I meant something else."

The wheel revolved one full turn. "What else?"

"I mean your time's coming."

"Now what in the devil are you talking about?"

"Well," he said, sounding very mature and wise, "one of these days you're going to look in the mirror, and you're going to see a girl a whole lot better-looking than Darlene on her best days." (Do you wonder why I love this prince among brothers?)

The wheel spun down to earth, and we dropped through the afternoon together, with the wind whistling in our ears. The midway of the Royal American Shows jumped up at us. Then we were planting our feet on solid ground.

Personally, I wouldn't have minded another ride.

chapter
five

Sherri was lurking in the back of my brain when I returned to school last fall. She'd recently appeared there. Fly-Me Sherri, the unidentified flying object who might just sweep out of the sky like a chicken hawk and carry off the best brother a sister ever had. I wondered how long I had to maintain silence about her, according to my promise to Hal at the reservoir. I can keep a secret, but I like to know how long.

In the front of my mind was Darlene. She'd become Miss Hybrid Seed Corn at the beginning of summer vacation. So she'd had no chance to be a school celebrity. Yet nobody could have avoided her stardom, emblazoned on every billboard in sight.

On the bus the first day I was contemplating these matters. Like what Darlene's fame would do to our group. Or, for that matter, what was it already doing to Darlene?

sixty-four

The big yellow Farmers' Express lumbered into Dunthorpe Central High School parking lot, Mrs. Bergschneider capably at the wheel. Over by the front steps I saw the group already assembled. To tell the truth, there were a lot of groups dotting the school yard, each regarding itself as the center of attention. I stepped off in the direction of My Own People.

Nearly everyone waiting for the doors to open was wearing shorts. There'd been a minor revolution in the spring over the Dunthorpe Central dress code. As their departing gesture, the seniors had spearheaded a campaign to make shorts legal for the first month back at school in the fall. For good measure, they added a tanktop amendment.

My concession to this new freedom was a pair of cut-off melon-colored denims, fringed by hand. I approached the group hoping my exposed thighs didn't look as floppy as Ludmilla's. "There she is, fresh from the fields," Ludmilla said by way of greeting.

Bernice flashed me a metallic smile of pure warmth and welcome.

"Hey, Verna," said Moon briefly, but nudged me in a comradely way.

And Darlene said, "Oh, hi," generally at me as if I might be her mother.

Casual reunions like ours were going on all over the schoolyard. Shrieks and hugs are out of place at school opening, which is supposed to be a National Day of Mourning. The only thing that set our group apart was Darlene.

Instead of wearing the new uniform, she had on a coy little red-and-white checked dress, nipped at the waist and scooped at the neck. We'd all seen it often. It was the number she'd worn in the corn poster. Above and below dress level was Darlene herself, golden and gorgeous. Her eyes were made up for some kind of lighting a lot more subtle than morning sun. Nobody clustered around her but us.

I thought this was peculiar and nearly said so. If the first-string football squad had borne her around the athletic field in triumph, I wouldn't have been a bit surprised. I didn't expect any of the other girls to be dropping her curtsies, but I did think they'd be throwing looks her way. They were all looking the other way.

The gates yawned, and we marched into first period. By considerable maneuvering, we five had managed to get ourselves placed in the same eleventh-grade English class.

Miss Castle is the teacher, a spacey and sweetly strange spinster. She's literally a lady of the old school who makes you feel you ought to have a polished apple to put on her desk. Wings of gray hair spring from each side of her small, pointed face. She wears white blouses and straight skirts. On the blackboard she'd written

A HEARTFELT WELCOME
TO THIS PROMISING NEW CROP OF JUNIORS

After a quick look, we all studied each other's bare knees in embarrassment. When the bell rang, Miss Castle gave her unthumbed new grade book a pat. Then with a little hop, she was suddenly perched on the front of her desk. Her tiny lace-up shoes cleared the floor and swung there.

"Welcome," she said, her eyes seeking contact with all of ours, "and again welcome. A thousand welcomes."

Happy Applegate on the back row groaned aloud. The rest of us stirred with discomfort.

"I have been glancing over the roster for the class in anticipation of this, our first meeting. Some of you I know. Some of us are strangers now, and what is a stranger but a future friend?"

She paused to let this notion sink in. The thought of the whole world bulging with future friends bore down on us all.

"In even the most cursory inspection of the class roll, however, I see that we have a celebrity in our midst."

There was another pause for full dramatic effect. I happened to be looking at an angle across the room at Kenny Chisolm. He was the only junior being scouted by the coach for the starting five of the basketball team. It was already a major item since football is only a ritual for us, and futile at that. Basketball is the Big Time and a year-round topic of speculation. Kenny's case was especially noteworthy since he's only five feet six inches high. But it's said that his potential as the fastest dribbler in the conference is nothing short of miraculous. He could dribble through the ankles of Wilt the Stilt himself, like a tiny tornado.

Kenny began to expand the minute Miss Castle said

the word *celebrity*. During her lengthy pause, he grew three inches, and a game little sportsman's smile spread across his face. He inhaled through one nostril.

"And that celebrity, as you all well know, is Darlene Hoffmeister!" Miss Castle's heels tapped out a little buck-and-wing rhythm on the side of her desk.

"Who?" said Happy Applegate from the back of the room.

Kenny Chisolm deflated suddenly. His head dropped, and he reached down one little leg to pull up his white athletic sock. I could see a vein throbbing in his temple.

"Yes indeed, Darlene Hoffmeister, of our own class, is Miss Hybrid Seed Corn!"

"Who?" came another voice, not Happy's.

And then another one, a female one, asking, "Who?" It became a chant. People who had known Darlene Hoffmeister since kindergarten were saying "Who?" And getting louder and louder about it. It seemed to go on forever.

Ludmilla shot me a glance. I could see Bernice too. Her hand was over her mouth. Moon was out of range. Darlene was directly behind me. And the class was who-ing her out of existence.

All the animals in the jungle had turned on Darlene. "Who?" asked Kenny Chisolm and turned to stare directly at her. "*Who?*"

The chorus died away slowly, dissolving into muttering chuckles, a nasty spattering of applause, and at least one really foul word. I could feel Darlene behind me, unmoving. I was frozen too, but I wanted to turn around. I don't know why. Just to make sure she knew I was with her and not against her, I guess. It was all so dumb. And so sudden. I turned and she was staring straight ahead. Her eyes didn't have their old vacant look. They glittered, and they comprehended everything. I gave her a little shrug, meant to say, "Don't let them get to you," but she was looking through me toward nothing.

Miss Castle was only mildly aware that something had misfired. She cleared her throat and looked vaguely around. Then she pressed on. "The honor conferred upon Darlene has a special significance to me, which I am very tempted to pass along to you boys and girls.

"Many years ago—oh, a great many I can assure you!—I was in my senior year of a teacher-training course at Okaw Valley State College. Of course in my day it was called the Okaw Valley Normal School. I have often thought how odd it was to call a college a normal school. Although I suppose we were all quite normal, ha ha."

No response from the class.

"Well, anyway, I was in my senior year there, and though you wouldn't think it to look at me today, who do you suppose was elected May Queen for our spring festival?"

"Who?" asked Happy Applegate. But the chorus wasn't taken up again.

"Yes, *I* was, and so I know the thrill that comes with an honor thus conferred."

More silence.

"Well, enough of this chatter," said Miss Castle. She slipped down to earth, straightened her skirt and walked kind of uncertainly back to her side of the desk. She sneaked a peek at her wristwatch.

We were on a shortened schedule that first day, thank heaven. And so there was just time for Miss Castle to give us our composition assignment. This met with the usual protesting moan, but by then most of us were glad enough to settle down to subject matter, except of course for Hap Applegate.

"Now I know you all expect the first writing assignment to be that old favorite, 'What I Did Last Summer.'" She tried to keep her voice sprightly, but the class had pretty well kicked the fight out of her. We'd managed to drain off her whole summer's build-up of enthusiasm in ten minutes. "But we must move with the times and find inspiration for our written expression in new topics, topics that point to the future ahead of us."

I thought briefly about the future ahead of Miss Castle. But it seemed too bleak.

"And so your first assignment will be this. . . ." She spun around to the blackboard, searched the length of the tray for chalk, found a piece on the floor instead, and wrote

MY HOPES, MY DREAMS

in sweeping letters right under her welcoming statement. Another groan rose out of the class.

"Yes," she said, turning around and smiling regardless. "*Your* hopes, *your* dreams. I don't want to say more. I want this writing to express *you* and the you you hope to be. Minimum of four paragraphs please, and watch your spelling."

"I ain't got any," Happy said.

"I beg your pardon. What is your name?" Only Miss Castle would have had to ask. Everybody knew Happy Applegate, dogged and determined quarterback and class dunce. Passing him was the annual faculty charity.

"Who me?"

"Yes."

"Applegate."

"Oh yes, August."

"Happy."

"Very well, Happy."

"I ain't got any."

"Any what, Aug—Happy?"

"Hopes and dreams."

"Oh, Happy, of course you do. You stand on the threshold of life, and deep within you—"

"I ain't got any hopes and dreams," Happy said firmly. The bell rang then. I thought it never would. We crowded out of the room. Dreamless, hopeless Happy brought up the rear.

The five of us met as usual at noon in the cafeteria. Who would dare invade our table? I'd thought all morning that if I were Darlene, I'd plan to have lunch in my locker. But she was there with a saucer of cottage cheese and some carrot sticks on her tray. We settled in silently. Too silently.

Ludmilla was chewing even when she didn't have anything in her mouth, and Moon was working through her franks and beans like something out of the barnyard. I turned my brain upside down to think of something to say. I was even tempted to break silence about Hal and Sherri as a neutral topic when Bernice suddenly wailed out, "Oh, Darlene, if you'd only worn shorts like everybody else, maybe—"

"I beg your pardon," said Darlene in her mother's voice. "Maybe what?"

"Well, maybe they wouldn't have been so nasty to you." Bernice was in anguish.

"Who do you mean?" said Darlene. For a minute I thought it was the old, slow Darlene who really didn't know.

"You know," Bernice said, "in English when—"

"She knows who you mean," Ludmilla said. "It isn't worth discussing."

"I could have told you to expect this kind of response," said Moon. "It's the adolescent mind. It refuses to tolerate hero-images that it doesn't create itself."

Darlene's eyes slipped out of focus, but she'd caught the general meaning.

Moon gestured at Darlene with her fork. "You left yourself open to attack, Darlene, the minute you—"

"She never left herself open to anything," Ludmilla

said. "It was her mother who entered her in that contest. Darlene's only the victim."

"Wait a minute, Moon," Bernice said, "let's go back to that about heroes and creation. Now do you mean if the kids around here had elected Darlene to something or other, then they wouldn't resent her?"

"Not exactly," said Moon, pushing her plate of franks and beans away, "because they never *would* have elected Darlene Homecoming Sweetheart or anything like that."

"But *why?*" wailed Bernice, giving Darlene a look as if she was our own personal side of prime beef.

"Because she really *is* the best-looking girl in the school. She puts everybody else out of the running. Don't you see, it wouldn't be a contest. I'll tell you who'd win a contest in this school—Beverly Fenster."

"Beverly Fenster?" Ludmilla and I yelped, entirely too loud. "Why?"

"Oh," Bernice said sadly, "her ankles are so *big.*"

"Nevertheless," Moon continued, "she's captain of the Pep Club Cheerleaders, but no better-looking than the rest of them. So the whole cheerleading team would promote her, and then they'd be her court of honor or something. And nobody'd feel threatened."

"We could be Darlene's court of honor," Bernice said, trying to miss the point.

"Please," Ludmilla said, "we're not the type."

The conversation had taken wing and flown away from Darlene. It was almost like the old days.

Over at Kenny Chisholm's table where the jocks all

sit to feed there were waves of boy-laughter. But nobody anywhere looked our way.

The plan for the rest of the day was to repair to Marquette Park right after school and do our Hopes and Dreams compositions together. It seemed by far the best way of getting that assignment out of the way.

I was luxuriating in newfound freedom. We'd all turned sixteen by last fall, so everybody had a driver's license. This was a bigger thing to town kids than to me. I'd been driving the truck to the Mount Yeomans grain elevator since I was thirteen without benefit of legality. In a pinch, I could have piloted the school bus if Mrs. Bergschneider had a stroke or something while at the wheel. But the point was, I could miss that bus, and one of the group would drive me home.

Moon and I met up with Ludmilla at her locker exactly at 3:45. Bernice dashed up a minute later, saying she'd seen Darlene leave school without even stopping at her locker. She'd yelled at her, but Darlene must not have heard.

We wandered out to the park, still dusty with its end-of-summer look. All the swings were empty, and there were shutters up on the frozen custard stand. When we settled at a picnic table in the shade, Ludmilla said, "Right, now let's not give this more than an hour."

"She said four paragraphs," Bernice sighed.

"Okay, that's fifteen minutes per paragraph. Let's get going."

"It's an impossible topic," Moon said, "and patronizing." She began to write immediately.

I didn't. Whenever the pen started toward the page, it couldn't put its point on a hope or a dream. After all, doesn't it take every bit of thought just to live in the present—or through it? I started to make that comment out loud, being unnerved by the scratching pens on three sides of me. But I was told to be quiet and write. So I did.

At 5:05, Ludmilla said, "Time's up."

"Oh wait," Bernice said, "just let me get to the end of this sentence."

We read our openings aloud, which is our usual way of winding up a group session. It's one of our rituals. Moon went first without being prompted. "'The hopes and dreams of the individual are meaningless in an increasingly impersonal and bureaucratic power structure. The very concept of freedom and—'"

"Okay," Ludmilla said, "that gives us an idea. Now you, Bernice." Bernice arranged her paper in front of her. "'My hopes and dreams are modest and few. To be a useful member of the community, to add my small store of—'"

"I like that about your small store," Ludmilla broke in, "considering your dad owns the biggest store in town." Bernice tittered.

"Now you, Verna."

"Who appointed you teacher?" I said. "You read next."

"All right. 'My hopes and dreams are bound up with the concept of a first-rate education. The future has need of men and women with a strong cultural—'"

"Fine," we all said.

"That's enough."

"Miss Castle will like that."

"*Now,* Verna."

I read, "'I have hopes for other people, but only dreams for myself, I guess.'" I stopped then, wishing they'd tell me that was enough. But they just sat there, waiting. I guess it wasn't a strong enough introductory sentence. "'I'd like to travel and see the world. I'd like to find out what life is like for other people I haven't ever seen. Maybe I'd even like to be one of them. But being practical, I am somewhat confused by dreams. I'm never sure what to do with them.' I'm not going to read any more," I told them. "It just goes on like that and it doesn't get anyplace."

"I didn't know you felt that way," Ludmilla said.

"I didn't either," I said.

"I wonder what Darlene will write," Bernice said.

Since Ludmilla lived nearest the park, we walked over to her house and watched her spend ten minutes backing their Chrysler Imperial out of the garage. Moon and I took the back seat. On the floor was a jack handle, an old mink furpiece, a bucket for live bait, and a paperback copy of Roget's *Thesaurus.* "My God," Moon said, staring between her knees, "it looks like the city dump down there."

We thundered off to the Steak-'n-Shake out on the General Pershing Highway for double-thick malteds. Ludmilla had said in the park she was hungry enough to eat acorns. We'd just brought the malteds back to the car when up drove a couple of station wagons, flanking us.

The entire football squad burst out, ready for their post-practice skimmed milk. These beefy ones scampered about in their summer work-out gear, white shorts and T-shirts that read "Dunthorpe Destroyers" across their chests. The drive-in was a mass of entangling, hairy legs and butting shoulders. The basic urge behind all this body contact makes you stop and think.

Out of them all came Wade R. Reynolds, and he made straight for our car. His father is Bernice's orthodontist, so she always turns her face away when he draws near. But he and Ludmilla have some sort of natural alliance. He plans to be the fourth generation of Reynoldses to go to Yale University in New Haven, Connecticut. This will find them both in the Ivy League if Ludmilla makes Vassar. Of course, these days, Wade could go to Vassar and Ludmilla could go to Yale, but that's all sort of out of my realm.

Wade doesn't have the football build, but then he doesn't need it since he's only the manager.

"Hey, Ludmilla."

"Hey, Wade. How's the team looking?"

"See for yourself," Wade said, all confidence and pride.

"I repeat," said Ludmilla, "how's the team looking?"

"Good, Ludmilla, very definitely good."

"Who's their first game with—Mount Yeomans?" (Girlish laughter from within the Chrysler Imperial.)

These pleasantries aside, Wade dropped his voice directly into Ludmilla's ear. Bernice retreated to the far end of the front seat and practically drank her malted from outside the window. Moon and I turned polite deaf ears and began rearranging the junk on the floor of the car with our sneaker-toes.

Suddenly Happy Applegate's huge head appeared at the back window on Moon's side, filling up the entire space.

"Hi, Moon."

"Hi, Hap."

"Where's the corn princess?"

Happy's great freckled face entered the car window as he pretended to search the floor for the delicious body of a young girl who might be lying there among the debris.

"If you mean Darlene," Moon said with menace, "she's not here."

"What happened? You throw her out of the club?"

"Oh no!" Bernice said.

"What club?" Moon said. Feeling the chill, Hap removed his head from the window Moon was already rolling up.

Wade withdrew from Ludmilla's window at the same time, giving her a crisp little wink and the thumbs-up sign. He slipped a notebook into the back pocket of his shorts. She reached for a cigarette. The presence of Wade always seems to make her light up. We all knew (because we'd all heard him) that Wade was booking up Ludmilla for the homecoming festivities. It was still seven weeks away, but Wade keeps a little calendar. He has no hopes and dreams for the future. He has plans.

"Lord God Almighty," Moon said, "Wade is so *earnest.*"

"Well, so are you, Moon," Ludmilla said through a smoke cloud.

"Maybe I am, but I've got priorities. With Wade every damn little thing is a business deal. He just signed you up for Homecoming like you were an insurance policy."

"It's insurance in a way," said Ludmilla coolly. "For both of us."

"Let's get off the subject of boys," I said, "or this car isn't going to be big enough to hold the four of us."

"Well, the only other topic is Darlene," Ludmilla said. "I heard Neanderthal Applegate back there talking. We're all identified with Darlene in the public mind—"

"The public doesn't have a mind," Moon said.

"—and she's beginning to show signs that might mean trouble."

"Yes," said Bernice, "we've got to stand by her and give her all our support."

"Now hold on one minute if you please," said Moon. "There's a slight absurdity at work in this car. Let's just take a good look at ourselves. Here we are, four female persons of your basic ordinary variety. And are we going to get ourselves in an uproar of concern over a girl picked out by nature and the seed corn company as the great sex symbol of our times?"

"So you're saying let's drop her?" Ludmilla asked.

"Did I say that?"

"You were getting there."

"Oh no, surely not! I didn't think Moon was getting there," Bernice said.

"Let's talk about boys," I said.

chapter
six

*W*e never did find out what Darlene's hopes and dreams were. She and Happy Applegate were the only ones who failed to hand in papers. Moon and Ludmilla got A's on theirs and had to read them out in class. Bernice and I got B minuses. My paper carried a sample of Miss Castle's handwriting, which read, *"Next time include more enriching and definite details to engage the reader and hold his interest."*

Miss Castle was pretty cut up about not getting a paper out of Darlene. It hurt her to have to put Darlene's name up on the board with Happy's. At the end of class Kenny Chisholm chalked a big heart around the two names, bringing a roar of joyous laughter from the departing crowd.

The weeks slipped by. On the dawn patrol of the chicken house I found myself gathering eggs with frost-nipped fingers. There were colors in the trees and cock

pheasants in the ditches. Dad worked like a demon com-
bining the beans and drilling the winter wheat before
the wet weather set in.

I wore Hal's old lumberjack shirt over a sweater to
school. Wade's football squad lost to Taylorville, Effing-
ham, Vandalia, Mattoon, Charleston, Clinton, Auburn,
and Hillsboro. Happy Applegate scored precisely twelve
points for the entire season.

The group had pretty well shrunk to four. Even when
Darlene was there, she was less there than before. She
still ate lunch with us, but would wander off by herself
after school. And she'd taken to dressing strangely, which
is not an easy thing to do in our society. Flowing purple
slacks and ankle-strap heels, silk blouses knotted at the
waist to let her stomach show through in a provocative
triangle. Parts of her were viewed appreciatively by certain elements of the school.

"She'll end up on the streets," Moon remarked one
time.

"You don't mean she'd quit school?" Bernice said,
aghast.

"No, Bernice, I mean something much, much worse."

"Oh *no!*" moaned Bernice.

In late October Darlene did a local TV commercial for
Midstates. They had her tricked out in a nurse's uniform
and cap. She was in a sterile hospital setting and bending
over an incubator. In it was a bunch of baby chicks, just
hatching out. All she had to do was look in the incubator,
look up at the camera, and smile confidently, then look

back at the incubator. Somebody else read the message about Midstates feeds. She was on every night with the weather report.

Soon after her debut, an anonymous poem appeared in the "What's Happening" column of the school newspaper:

> Who's on television, laying nightly eggs?
> Darling Darlene with her prize-winning legs!
>
> Who's the chickies' nursemaid on the silver screen?
> Darling Darlene, the corn-fed queen!

Beverly Fenster was elected Homecoming Sweetheart. She reigned from the top of a hay frame, surrounded by her Pep Club court of cheerleaders. They all carried their game-time pompoms and wore their regulation pleated skirts and letter sweaters.

Beverly saw fit to preside in a white net, ankle-covering formal and a rhinestone tiara. There's nothing much wrong with Beverly except she has too much bounce. She grinned without ceasing and seemed ever ready to leap up to lead her favorite cheer, which is

> Minnesota pine tree! Arizona cactus!
> Dunthorpe plays YOUR team for practice!

This may provide a clue as to who wrote the anonymous newspaper poem. We lost to Centralia, seven to nothing. But the victory dance went on anyway that Saturday night in the school parking lot. Bernice and I were dateless but decided to brazen it out and go. We

stood around watching the couples gyrate and the spotlight catching Beverly's grin.

Wade and Ludmilla swept by. Wade was doing the box
step to the electronic-Afro rhythms of a local group,
"The Brethren of Despair." Ludmilla looked like she'd
had to die in order to collect on her insurance policy.

Moon was completely involved with a college boy
she'd met at her summer-school course. He was wearing
a dashiki and thongs. She had on a burlap caftan and
ceramic jewelry. They conversed while lunging to the
beat.

"Gee," said Bernice, "they look just like the pictures
in the Bible," which is as close as she ever gets to a snide
comment.

About the time I was willing to call it a night, Darlene
stepped out of the shadows at the far end of the parking
lot. It was like seeing her ghost. She'd been out of school
for a whole week, and nobody knew why. We'd tried
to call her, but there wasn't anybody at home. Actually,
we only tried once.

Darlene's age level seemed to have jumped seven or
eight years. She was wearing a wool suit with fur at the
cuffs and a real orchid on her lapel. With her was a guy
in a plaid sport coat and turtleneck. She was smiling over
her shoulder and giving him her you-are-my-very-
own-stand-of-seed-corn look.

They stood at the edge of the light, keeping their
distance. But they were in full view, as I suppose Darlene
wanted to be. At first I couldn't figure who the guy was.

eighty-four

Older, naturally. Something familiar about him. Recollection was creeping over me in interesting stages.

Bernice spotted them. "Oh, I wonder who he is?"

"Never saw him before in my life," I lied.

I'd seen lots of him. He'd been the man in Mrs. Hoffmeister's bed.

Darlene was back in school on the Monday after Homecoming. That morning in homeroom Ludmilla, Moon, Bernice, and I all got green slips. These are summonses to appear at the counselor's office without delay. We all exchanged dark looks. Obviously the group was being rounded up.

On the way down the hall, Ludmilla said, "For Pete's sake keep cool. This isn't a raid. We haven't done anything."

Wondering what we'd done, we entered Miss Schuster's office. She was wearing her uniform—a shirtwaist dress and a leather strap on her wristwatch. Penny loafers peered out from under her desk. "Hello, girls. Sit down. Relax. I mean that sincerely." She slapped her desk with the flat of her hand. Bernice shied like a colt.

"I'll come to the point. The reason I've called you all in here together is that I could use your help. It's my job to see trouble brewing, and I see it." She searched our faces for positive response and didn't find any.

"I'm aware that you're all friends of Darlene Hoffmeister." We settled back cautiously. "And so I'm going to speak frankly. Gradewise, Darlene has never been up to topflight achievement. However, she's been able to keep her nose above water in the past. This year I'm not so sure.

"And point number two. Darlene doesn't have a particularly well-defined character. But it's been my intuitive feeling that in the past you've exercised a positive supportive influence on her. . . ."

This was meant to draw us all over on Miss Schuster's side of the desk, so to speak. But if she was any judge of human nature, she could've seen the hackles rising all around her. "Now I'm not so sure. The kind of attention Darlene is receiving publicity-wise these days is enough to turn the head of a girl with a much more stable value system than Darlene possesses."

All this affected us in the opposite direction of Miss Schuster's intentions. Our ranks closed against her.

"Darlene's values are her own business, Miss Schuster," Ludmilla said, giving her a level glance.

This slowed Miss Schuster down a bit, but she continued, "Yes, but it seems to me that the influence of positive peer-group pressure can work—"

"Peer-group pressure is for street gangs and the locker room," Moon said. "We're subjected to enough pressure from the adult authority establishment as it is without manipulating each other."

Miss Schuster sat there dumfounded, as if one of her old college textbooks had jumped off the shelf and turned on her.

"And besides, what could we *do?*" asked Bernice.

This seemed to finish off Miss Schuster. "Well, I don't know," she said in a small voice. "I thought maybe you'd have some ideas. I thought maybe you'd have some plans we could kick around just among ourselves. . . ." She tapered off and fumbled inside her desk for something. Out came a Sunday edition of the St. Louis paper. Spreading it so we could all see it, she said, "This will probably be in the Dunthorpe papers today." Then she retreated.

A headline announced that Darlene had been named Central United States Teen Super Doll. There was a picture of last year's retiring monarch placing the crown on her head. Darlene was wearing a swim suit, a wrap with ermine tails, her smile, and the orchid I'd seen on her Saturday night. Under the picture it said:

> Miss Darlene Hoffmeister, 17, of Dunthorpe, named winner in regional Teen Super Doll competition at St. Louis Civic Auditorium Friday night. Formerly Miss Hybrid Seed Corn, the blonde, bewitching, blue-eyed beauty (35-22-35) will make a midwinter public-relations tour of New York City media centers and will later compete against other regional Teen Super Dolls for the national title at a contest to be held next summer in Las Vegas.
>
> Asked her reaction, the successful contestant said she was "honored."

"Hell," Ludmilla said, "she's not seventeen."

"That's just the sort of thing I mean," said Miss Schuster eagerly. "She's rushing her fences. She's trying to grow up too—"

"Hush," Moon said. "We're not through reading this."

Miss Schuster subsided meekly. But she tried again by saying, "Well, there you have it. And it seems to me that we could all do her a great service by—"

"Leaving her alone," Ludmilla said.

Moon cleared her throat. "Miss Schuster, I don't much feel like discussing Darlene's academic future behind her back. But just for the sake of argument, would you say she's college material?"

"Oh no, that is, maybe. I mean if she'd knuckle down and . . . and—"

"Conform?" Moon suggested dangerously.

"Well, yes, conform for one thing. Conformity is not a dirty word. And there's such a thing as a late bloomer."

"Miss Schuster," I said, "Darlene bloomed before any of us."

"Oh yes," Bernice put in, "in her own way she did."

"And this is her way," Ludmilla said, more to us than to Miss Schuster. "The kids around here are jealous of her and snotty about it. They sneer at her every chance they get." She turned suddenly to Miss Schuster. "Why should she even want to bother with this place as long as she's getting the kind of attention she can get somewhere else? I wouldn't give it up if I was her—were she. I'd tell this whole school they could—"

"That will do," said Miss Schuster, running both hands through her very short hair. "I've kept you girls from class too long as it is. Run along and . . . and give this some serious thought." She whirled in her chair and lunged for a cabinet to pull the file on the next patient.

eighty-eight

There are two things wrong with guidance counselors. They're always trying to nip something in the bud that's already gone to seed. And they're forever trying to get somebody to do their work for them.

"I think we're pretty great when we have to rise to an occasion," Ludmilla said as we stepped off down the hall. She spoke too soon.

We'd grown used to lunch-time Darlene deteriorating from silent to sullen to vanished completely. From the very beginning we'd been talking around her like she was an elderly, deaf relative. That noon she was already at the cafeteria table before we arrived. There was definitely blood in her eye.

She didn't let us settle in before she said, "What were you four called into the counselor about?" This sent the troops scurrying for cover. Who'd have thought she'd notice?

"Well," said Ludmilla, "well, it was about . . . Advanced Placement History."

"Don't lie," said Moon.

"No, don't," said Bernice. "It was about you, Darlene."

(Groans.)

"What about me?" Darlene snapped, staring at all of us. She had purple shading under her eyes and frosty white over them. False lashes too. The effect should have been ridiculous. But somehow it put the fear of God into us all. Talk about the Evil Eye.

"Miss Schuster told us about you being crowned Central United States Teen Super Doll," I said, playing for time.

"Yes, that's right," Bernice said. "Congratulations—again."

"Knock it off," Darlene said (Lord, she was getting brittle). "She didn't call you in there just to tell you that."

"I wish you'd told us yourself, Darlene," Ludmilla said. "That's big news. It's . . . great."

"Look," said Darlene. "My mother got permission from the attendance office for me to be out of school last week to go down there to St. Louis. It was my business and nobody else's."

"That's more or less what we told Miss Schuster," Ludmilla said quietly.

"Well I'm glad you did," Darlene said, "*if* you did." We let that pass. If it was a staring contest, Darlene lost. She looked away, and nobody said anything.

When she spoke again, it was in her little-girl voice. For old times' sake, it was nice to hear it again, the tone of it at least. "Look, I know what I'm doing. I don't need . . . I don't need—"

"You don't need us," Ludmilla finished for her. "That's about what we told Miss Schuster too."

"You did?" she looked at all of us. I never saw such a lonely look.

"Yes," Bernice said, "I guess we did really."

"Well, that's all right then," she said, and her voice wobbled. She got up then and walked away. At the end of the lunch period Bernice carried Darlene's tray back to the kitchen for her.

chapter

seven

On the first day of the Christmas holiday, Hal and I were out early, looking for holly in the hedgerows. Not finding any, we raided the Mount Yeomans cemetery for boughs off the ornamental firs.

As we strolled boldly away through the tombstones with our Yuletide harvest, I decided to take the bull by the horns. "Look, is it on or off?"

"What?"

"You know what. Sherri. Are you or aren't you? Is she or isn't she? Will she or won't she? Et cetera."

Hal kept on trudging, stubbing his boot toes up against the tufts of brown grass.

"Far be it from me to poke my nose in and like that," I explained, "but I'm getting a little tired of waiting. Aren't you?" I had the bleak feeling that Ludmilla would have been able to handle him better.

"If you two are thinking about big plans come next

summer after graduation, seems like there wouldn't have to be any dark secret at this late date."

I knew I was pushing, but with brothers sometimes you have to. I also didn't seem to be getting any place at all. Something about a graveyard makes people tight-lipped. Other people, not me.

"I was hoping you'd bring her here at Christmas. Is she at home with her folks?"

That seemed to do it. Hal said, "No, she hasn't got any folks. Besides, she's got three turnarounds to Curaçao."

"She's got what?"

"She has to work. Fly down and back to Curaçao three times right through Christmas day."

"What's Cura—whatever?"

"It's a place down in the Caribbean Sea. A tourist place, I guess."

"Oh."

Hal was pacing it off pretty brisk down the road toward home. It was taking most of my breath just to keep abreast of him. But I was thinking. Young love makes you shy, even shifty, they tell me. Hal seemed to be carrying it pretty far though. Anyway, I thought I ought to know what there was to know. What good is keeping a secret for months without knowing the particulars of it? I decided he wished he hadn't said anything to me out at Persimmon Woods back in the summer.

"Where does she live?"

"All over the place like stewardesses do. But she's based

in New York and works out of there. She's in different towns a lot, different countries even. They put them up wherever they happen to be."

"A regular gypsy. I can't visualize the life."

"Neither can I."

"When do you get to see each other?"

"She can bid on the flights she wants to work and gets her choice some of the time. She flies out to Indianapolis, and I go down and meet her there."

"She has an Indianapolis turnaround, does she?" I remarked knowledgeably. We were down by the mail box then and turning into the lane. Hal would soon be making his escape down to the barn or someplace. Time was short, making me bold. "What's the problem?"

"Oh well," he said, shaking his handsome head, "It's hard to try to work everything out. I don't know why she'd be willing to settle for me. She's been everywhere and meets a lot of interesting . . . people. Eats her meals in hotels and all that kind of thing. What am I but a hayseed—"

"Watch that kind of talk," I warned him, sounding severe. "There's nothing wrong with the way we live."

"I know it. You know I know it," he said, giving a swipe at the fence post with his load of greens. "I didn't mean—"

"And besides," I said. "You're going to be a doctor. You're going to go to medical school and be a rich and healing doctor. What girl in her senses wouldn't—"

"That's enough, Verna," Hal said. And the tone of his

voice made me know he meant it. But I was still trying
to think of something to keep him going. We might be
getting someplace with this conversation, I thought. And
maybe getting him good and irritated might be a way.

But we both noticed a car pulled up by the front gate.
It looked familiar, but I couldn't place it. With great
relief, Hal said, "Company," and hotfooted it off in the
direction of the implement shed.

I went up to the house and heaped the greens on the
porch. Time enough later to arrange them artistically on
the mantel so that Aunt Eunice could spend the holidays
complaining about shedding needles.

Voices and the smell of coffee drifted in from the
dining room. I walked in there and nearly swooned with
surprise. There sat Mama and Mrs. Hoffmeister nose-to-
nose at the table, drinking coffee out of the good cups.

Mrs. Hoffmeister was making her second unscheduled
appearance down on the farm. This time in a fur coat,
thrown back over her chair. Otherwise, she was a sym-
phony of classy tailoring in her favorite shade. She
seemed intent upon selling Mama a bill of goods on some
subject or other. Mama wasn't dressed for company. She
looked medium agonized, but attentive. They very nearly
missed my entrance.

"Oh, Verna," Mama said, distracted. "look who's
here." (Who could miss her?) But Darlene wasn't along.
I hadn't seen her except in passing and occasionally behind me in Miss Castle's class since that last day in the
cafeteria, more than a month before.

Mrs. Hoffmeister gave me an overwhelming greeting and slipped into her furs. She was beating a rather hasty retreat, and her parting words to Mama were, "I hope you'll give this some *very* serious thought, Mrs. Henderson, because naturally time is of the essence. I feel sure you'll agree with me that this is a truly *extraordinary* opportunity." With that she was gone.

But she hadn't cleared the front gate before Aunt Eunice appeared. She'd been right there on the kitchen side of the door the whole time.

She marched on Mama and burst into speech, "I'm not going to say but one thing to you, Edith. Just one thing. And you know I never meddle. But here's what I have to say: NO, Edith, positively NO. It's the most harebrained thing that ever I heard tell of, and don't so much as entertain the thought of it!"

Veins and tendons were standing out in Aunt Eunice's neck. She swept back into the kitchen. I was eaten alive with curiosity. "Mama, what—"

"Verna, wait. Just wait. Till your dad and Hal come in for their dinner. Then maybe we can get things worked out."

"But—"

"Verna, please! The morning's not half over, and I'm worn out." She looked it too.

Waiting for dinner was awful. It didn't start out too well either. For one thing, I imagined that Hal was eyeing me for fear I'd blurt out his Sherri-secret, as if I would.

Aunt Eunice was up on the edge of her chair and ready

to snap. Mama looked plain worried. About the only conversation there was came from Dad, which didn't amount to much more than asking the blessing. "Car in the lane this morning," he said finally. "Who was it?"

I could see Mama was going to be slow taking that up, so I said, "It was Mrs. Hoffmeister, Darlene's mother."

"Just paying a call?"

"Well, not exactly," Mama said. "It was the funniest thing."

"Funny?" Aunt Eunice said. "I should say it wasn't!"

"Well, you know, she was telling about how Darlene won Central United States Teen Super Doll at the pageant down in St. Louis. I guess that was something! She's so proud of her, you know. And Darlene won so many lovely things, I guess. A dinner ring with a real opal in it and a shoe and sweater wardrobe and a full set of sterling silver flatware. In the Rambler Rose pattern." It's not like Mama to beat around the bush. It was all I could do to keep from jumping up and screaming. Aunt Eunice seemed to feel the same way. "And, ah, part of the duties Darlene has for being a Super Doll is this three-day trip they're giving her to New York City. Oh, I guess she's going to be on a television show, and I don't know what all.

"She's going the day after Christmas, so she won't be missing school or anything like that. . . . And of course Mrs. Hoffmeister's just real excited about it. Anybody would be, I guess. . . ."

"Edith," Aunt Eunice said, sounding exasperated.

"Well now, Eunice, I'm telling this. Mrs. Hoffmeister talked to *me,* you know. You weren't in the room at the time." That put a rare damper on Aunt Eunice, for the time being at least. "Well anyway, where was I?"

Hal was beginning to follow this with interest. And something unfamiliar was coming over me. Mama shifted gears and went on, "It seems like the people who manage the Super Doll business say Darlene can take somebody along with her on this trip to New York City. All expenses paid."

"Isn't her mother going with her?" Hal asked.

"That's just it. She can't. She has something else she has to do, and she can't get away. She didn't say what. But the thing is, the Super Doll can take along a friend anyway. Another girl, I mean."

Mama looked at me. Then they were all looking at me. Except for Aunt Eunice who was looking at the ceiling with her whole face pulled up into a prune.

I don't know what went through my mind first. Nothing probably. The eyes of your family on you tend to slow down thinking. But then a big rush of thoughts all cropped up at the same time. Me going to New York City? I couldn't believe it. And *why* me? Who'd taken the notion to ask me? Surely not Darlene. She couldn't have given me a thought in over a month. And very little thought before that.

It must have been her mother. I'd have bet a dollar she didn't even know Darlene wasn't running around with us anymore. Mama didn't know that herself. But

me in New York City. It didn't make any sense. And
with one word I could have solved the whole thing right
there.

Because then I knew what Aunt Eunice had meant . . .
*NO, Edith, positively NO. It's the most harebrained thing
that ever I heard tell of.* . . . All I had to do was agree
with Aunt Eunice. Agree with Aunt Eunice? That'll be
the day.

But what was I supposed to do in New York City?
Keep an eye on Darlene, I supposed. Now there's a job
and a half. Harebrained was the word for it. But something in the back of my mind came forth. The B minus
Hopes and Dreams theme for Miss Castle. How I'd written that I'd like to see the world and other people and
all that.

Then the big hot wave of wishing washed over me.
If I didn't get to go to New York City with Super Doll
Hoffmeister, I'd as soon die. For all I knew, I was upstairs
packing that very minute.

But we were still at the table. Mama and Dad were
looking at me, waiting for me to say something. Aunt
Eunice was waiting too, to say something herself. And
Hal seemed to be having thoughts of his own.

"Well," Dad said after a while, "that sure is something."

"Yes," Mama said, quavering, "Mrs. Hoffmeister says
it's the opportunity of a lifetime and Darlene would be
real glad for the company. And there's to be strict chap-
eroning. And it *is* only three days." Mama's voice was

getting weaker, but I was still picking up the signals. "Of course, one thing about it is, they have to fly. That's the only way to get there. But they'll see so many wonderful things. It'd be educational. . . ."

"Educational?" Aunt Eunice put in, "I'd hate to think what kind of an education! An education in New York City? Do you know what kind of things go on in a place like that?"

"Well, no, I don't, Eunice," Dad said unexpectedly. "Do you?"

"No, I don't, and what's more I don't want to. Why, what business do two young girls have sashaying all the way across the country on a moment's notice? And at Christmastime too. Why we don't even know anybody at New York City."

"Yes we do," Hal said. "I do."

For the first time in my life, if not the last, I felt like Darlene. Everybody was talking around me. They all three turned to Hal then, Aunt Eunice looking suspicious and betrayed.

"Who do you know there, Hal?" Mama said. "Somebody at college?" If I hadn't been in such a turmoil, I'd have enjoyed that. Hal had spoken before he meant to.

"Not exactly. It's a girl I know there. She'd look in on Verna while she was there. I mean if Verna wants to go."

He wasn't going to get off with that. Mama's eyes lit up. She knew she was going to find out what she'd been waiting to hear. "Well, tell us about her, Hal. We're all ears." (Were they ever!)

"Her name's Sherri McDonald, and we're . . . we're pretty good friends."

"There's McDonalds living over by Stonington, but she wouldn't be one of them," Aunt Eunice said, ruling Sherri out.

"Is she a special friend of yours, Hal?" Mama said, trying to make it as easy on him as she could. Dad was beginning to smile a little.

"Yes, she's . . . special." Boy if I ever saw anybody who wanted to be somewhere else, there he sat.

"What does she do in New York City?"

"She's an airline stewardess."

"Well I never!" Mama said.

"Neither did I," said Aunt Eunice.

Nothing was settled at the dinner table. Whatever is when a whole family's involved? And I hadn't actually opened my mouth. I had sense enough to know that the less I said and the more Aunt Eunice said, the better the chances would be. Besides, whether they knew it or not, my mind was already halfway to New York City.

It was later when Aunt Eunice had gone off to her room to wash her hands of the whole business. I was at the drainboard polishing the company silver for Christmas dinner. Mama was at the kitchen table, picking out nutmeats.

I was still being as silent as the tomb, which is really never a bad idea. And Mama began to talk. It was almost thinking out loud, and she never stopped with her work. "There's always lots of things to consider when something unexpected comes up," she said. "You know, Verna, I never have been anyplace in my life. Oh your dad and I were over to Des Moines one time years ago. But I didn't care anything about it. I'd as soon have been at home the whole time. I didn't know what I was seeing, I guess.

"You're different, Verna. Going to school in town and all that. But then you were always going to be different, I could see that.

"You know how it is though, everything comes at once. Like this noon, I thought we were getting you sorted out, and then Hal came out with something. It's kind of—I don't know—it's kind of like you're both just picking up and going. It's sudden.

"Well, it isn't like the end of the world. You'll be—you'd be back in a few days. And I know it isn't anything too definite about Hal. And he's grown up and I know he'll do what he thinks best."

She was working a little harder with the nutmeats then. A mountain of walnut shells was growing beside her. "And in a couple of years you'll be eighteen. Why that's old enough to vote these days. And you'll be in college, I hope.

"I tell you the truth, Verna . . . I, I'd keep you both home with us all together if I had my way. But that doesn't work. You have to go out and see for yourself and learn to make your own way. I didn't set the rules, but there they are.

"Aunt Eunice doesn't understand that. And I'm not altogether sure your dad does either. He doesn't say much, but I've seen him looking at the both of you like he wanted to put bricks on your heads to keep you from growing up. Men are that way. They fear change worse than we do. Why, Hal's scared about his future right now, and you and I can both see it, can't we?"

I nodded.

"There's another thing too about this . . . opportunity for you. I wouldn't even waste my breath saying it around Eunice. But I think it'd be a good thing for you to go along to New York City with Darlene. Her mother talks like everything is just perfect and couldn't be improved upon. But do you know, I don't think she's so sure. I think it would put her mind at ease if you went along with Darlene. Mrs. Hoffmeister's a good talker, but I'm telling you she has worries about her daughter I don't have about you."

It was the longest speech I ever heard Mama make. She was waiting then for me to tell her what I was going to do.

"Well, Mama, what with looking after Darlene and looking over Sherri, it seems like I can't stay home."

She scooped up her walnut shells onto a newspaper and wadded it up to stick in the stove. "They tell me there are plenty of high buildings in New York City, but I know you'll keep both feet on the ground," she said. "And you can leave your Aunt Eunice to me."

chapter
eight

Christmas day came and went. It was the usual flutter of tissue paper, satin bows to be saved for next year's wrapping, and all the cousins arriving for dinner. But my mind wasn't on it.

As somebody's last-minute purchase, I got a leatherette flight bag—from "Santa Claus." (We keep up all the traditions.) On Christmas night I got down to serious packing, a first in my life. Since I was pretty sure I wouldn't sleep, I planned to pack till morning. Hal let me use his big suitcase, so I was putting everything into that and my new bag. Then I was taking it all out and starting fresh.

Mama had been on the phone three different times with Mrs. Hoffmeister. I thought it was Darlene's place to call me too. But I knew she wouldn't. And I thought it was just as well. If she didn't want me tagging along, I'd just as soon not know it.

I seriously considered calling one or all of the group
to tell them of this startling turn of events. But I thought
a postcard mailed from New York City would be more
sensational. Besides, I didn't want any advice.

Mama came up to my room and hovered around the
bed where I had everything in and out of the cases. "You
figure you'll have the right clothes?"

"Well, Mama, it won't be me they'll be looking at.'"

"Take plenty of warm things." She wanted to help,
but the sight of that suitcase yawning open on the bed
was too much for her. She went on downstairs.

What with Christmas and packing, I was so tired I
nearly went to sleep crossways in the bed with my clothes
on. All night long I dreamed that Darlene and I were
flying on an airplane straight toward a mountain. The
pilot was Captain Sherri McDonald. Just before the crash,
Darlene handed me a golden crown. "Here," she said,
"YOU be the Super Doll. I don't want to be it anymore."

We were to meet Darlene and her mother at Dunthorpe Municipal Airport where there's a plane a day
to the East. I thought sure we'd miss the flight because
we got a late start. Aunt Eunice had to be coaxed at the
last minute. She said she didn't have any business at any
airport. And besides, you couldn't just turn your back
on property.

We made it with minutes to spare. By the time the
control tower loomed up, my feet were plenty cold. I
wanted Mama and Dad to say they couldn't do without

me. But Dad was looking for the entrance to the parking lot, and Mama was staring at the airport like it was Sodom and Gomorrah combined. I wanted Hal to get protective. What good's a college education if it doesn't teach you how to take care of your loved ones? But no, he was asking me to check my purse again to make sure I had Sherri's address in case she couldn't get through to me at the hotel. *At the hotel.* Good grief, I never stayed in a hotel in my life. Why start now?

The Hoffmeisters' car was in the parking lot. They'd gone on into the airport, but there was somebody sitting in it. Their all-purpose man. The one who went to homecoming with Darlene and to bed with her mother.

We walked right past him without anybody else noticing. He was sitting there in the back seat deeply engrossed in a copy of the *Reader's Digest.*

The plane from Sioux City to La Guardia Airport in New York was on time according to the announcements board and Mrs. Hoffmeister. Her presence filled up the whole place. The businessmen waiting for the plane divided their eyes between Hoffmeister mother and Hoffmeister daughter.

"Oh, why, Verna, hello!" Darlene said to me in a ringing, well-toned voice. "Isn't it *absolutely thrilling?*" But she tried to look utterly bored when she said it, and she was obviously working from a script. Super Doll doing her stuff. For one awful second I thought she was going to give me a sisterly embrace. Though those eyes of hers were made up to look like perpetual surprise, she gave me a sharp once-over with them. I guess I looked mousy enough to pass inspection.

The truth is, I was looking her over too. The wave in the hair, the new long line of the eyebrow, the winter coat over the arm that matched the understated suit. The clunky little businesswoman-type shoes with the stacked heels. Oh yes, she was well out of the chicken feed stage. And heading fast for the cover of *Ingenue,* or better yet, *Seventeen.*

They called the plane then, and the passengers lined up at a counter to be searched for bombs or anything dangerous they might be packing.

"What in this world are they doing to those people?" Aunt Eunice said, her eyes abulge. Pretty soon they were searching me and my Santa Claus bag too. I was in the line with my boarding pass before I realized we were on our way. It hadn't dawned on me that I couldn't turn back and really say goodbye. But maybe it was just as well.

After the weapon search, Darlene and I turned around. She gave a rather stagy wave over the barricade in her mother's direction and a real toothpaste ad of a smile. I looked at the huddle of Hendersons. Mama had her hand up to her mouth. And Aunt Eunice . . . Aunt Eunice was stalking right up to the airline official who'd searched us. Then she was having words with him. I wanted to bolt out onto the runway. But I couldn't move. Neither could the airline official. She was past him and right up to me before he knew it.

"Here," she said, putting something round and cold into my hand. "I mean you to have it before. Use it and think of me. Now get on out there before they leave you behind."

She gave me a shove, and I was walking across the runway behind Darlene toward the biggest, loudest, closest airplane of my experience. At the foot of the steps, I opened my hand to see what Aunt Eunice had put there. It was a purse flagon of Miss Misty perfume. One of her prize possessions. I turned around and waved then. I waved and waved.

The first airline stewardess I ever saw wasn't Sherri McDonald. It was Esther, according to her nametag. She welcomed Darlene with one of Darlene's own smiles. It was a regular battle of the ivories.

Flying to New York City with Darlene was like sharing a seat—five miles up—with three people. The Darlene of the dear old days who squeaked with terror when Esther-the-stewardess told us which exit to jump out of during the emergency we weren't going to have anyway. Then there was the Darlene of the present, sipping complimentary fruit juice in a cocktail party kind of way and regarding me like the hired girl. And then there were the glimpses of some future Darlene.

This creature came to light a couple of hours later when we were slanting in over New York City. She'd forgotten me and was looking down on the town like it was spread out at her feet especially to do her homage.

I made myself look past her out the window too. There were all those buildings pointing up through the haze and the rivers full of barges and the bridges so strong and graceful. And helicopters like dragonflies. It was such a picture, I forgot to be afraid.

But in the blank spaces where the little cloud puffs got in the way, I could see other things. I thought I caught a glimpse of Hal and Dad out in the pasture burning brush. And Mama and Aunt Eunice working the Christmas dinner remains over into a second-day casserole. All I could think of was that I was a thousand miles too far from them.

In New York when you get off a plane, you walk straight into the airport without touching ground. I knew Darlene was expecting a brass band and the mayor.

Instead, a funny little woman with black hair and horn rims came jangling up to us. She had on such an assortment of charms, chains, and bangles that I wondered how her frame supported the weight. As a backdrop for all this metalwork, she had on a sort of leotard costume and a fuzzy fake fur coat. It was only the day after Christmas, but she was already in training for Halloween. She looked the pair of us over and said, "Miss Hoffmeister?" but not really to either one of us. More between us.

Darlene didn't care much for that and identified herself pretty quick. Since she wasn't going to introduce me, I did it myself. The lady told us she was Miss Teal "from the agency," and that she was sorry as she could be that the vice-president of the agency couldn't be here himself, but we'd be seeing him in the evening. She said she was in charge of us.

We weren't out of the airport before I'd seen more people in a hurry than I ever had in my life. Our suitcases came down of their own accord on a chute and went in a circle till we took them off. Everything in the place was in a state of perpetual motion.

Out at the curb was a big black Lincoln limousine, drawn up for us. You could tell that was more the thing Darlene had in mind. There was a chauffeur too, in a cap. And off we glided, Miss Teal between us in the back seat. She began to explain about out itinerary and our schedule of "commitments." I doubt if Darlene took in any of it.

I know I didn't because my eyes were glued to the window. We were shooting along a highway through the biggest cemetery I ever saw. On both sides were thousands upon thousands of tombstones, jammed right up flush with each other. There wouldn't have been room to breathe, not that it matters. Awful, tacky plastic Christmas wreaths were leaning up on some of the stones, and the wind was whipping their ribbons. I hadn't known what to expect from New York City people, but I sure never knew most of them were dead.

Then right away we were getting to the live part. Miss Teal pointed out the Chrysler Building and the United Nations. Before we could see them though we were in a tunnel. Then we were out, and the walls of all the houses moved in on us, close as tombstones.

Our hotel was the Regal Park Towers. From the first hour to the last I never saw the top of it. It reached right up into the clouds. The whole city did. It would have made anybody but Darlene feel small.

At first I thought Miss Teal was mad at us. When she wasn't barking, everything she said seemed to be routed through her nose. "Now lissen here, I'm gonna tell you something," she'd say and grab us both by the coat sleeve. Then she'd tell whatever it was—turning in our keys when we left the hotel and keeping a good grip on our purses at all times. She wasn't really mad at us at all. It was just the way she talked. Like a lady gangster. It was the way almost everybody talked there. Loud, right out of the nose, and fast. Like they were all afraid you might try to get a word in edgewise. But she didn't have a worry in the world there. Neither Darlene nor I could think of a thing to say.

She got us checked in, and a bellboy took our luggage up to the room. He had a face like a rat, including the whiskers. And when Miss Teal sent him on his way, she gave him folding money for a tip. I could have fainted.

But Miss Teal was a regular strongbox of money. She gave Darlene and me both a hundred dollars cash for "incidentals." At the time I thought that was enough incidentals to see me through to summer.

While Miss Teal was getting us settled, she said she'd take a room on the same floor of the hotel if we wanted her to. But if we thought we could manage, she'd as soon go home to her own place. It seemed she lived in an apartment with a poodle dog, and she felt better if she was at home to walk it regularly.

For a minute I couldn't think why you'd have to help a dog take a walk. I guess about everybody in New York City keeps livestock, which is a terrible headache for them. She was making for the door then, and I was glad to see her go because she tended to address her remarks more to me than to Darlene.

"Now lissen," she said, "take my advice and get rested up. Your first engagement isn't until dinner this evening. And learn from me—when I leave, shoot the bolt and put the chain on the door. You gotta watch yourself every minute. If you want anything, ring for room service."

Then she was gone. Miss Teal was New York City's version of Aunt Eunice. Neither one of them felt right about turning their back on property. As for ringing up room service, if it meant the return of Rat Face, I for one could do without.

With the bolt shot and the chain hung, claustrophobia swept over me. It was like being locked in the tower with Rapunzel. Ivy suddenly growing up over the door wouldn't have surprised me a bit. A nice enough prison, though. Big daisies on the wallpaper with spreads to match on two big beds. And space left over for lots of furniture and a big color TV. There was a floor-to-ceiling window, but all you could see from it was cloud or smoke or both.

On the coffee table there was a spray of hothouse roses.

Darlene was cooing over them. I read the card over her shoulder:

NEW YORK
and the
INTERNATIONAL TALENT UNLIMITED AGENCY
WELCOME CENTRAL UNITED STATES TEEN SUPER DOLL
"She walks in beauty like the night"

"Isn't it *divine?*" Darlene said, turning to address my forehead. "Isn't it simply *lovely* of them?"

"Darlene," I said to her eyes, "look, it's me, Verna."

"What?"

"It's me, Darlene—Relax."

"What?"

"The chain's on the door. It's just the two of us. Save the act for later."

Her eyes narrowed. "I knew it. I knew it'd be a drag with you along. It was Mother's—"

"Don't think I don't know it. And I know that according to the terms of the offer, you could bring a friend along. And I also know you don't particularly figure I'm a friend of yours anymore. But I'm along."

"So I see," she said. "And I see something else too. You're *jealous*. You're like the rest of them. You just can't stand it, can you?"

"What? Your act?"

"You know what I mean. You just can't stand it because I'm . . . because I have some—advantages you don't have."

"Would you believe it if I told you I'm glad for you?"

"Are you kidding? I told you, you're just like the rest of them. You'd stab me in the back if you could."

"Well, turn around."

"Very funny. Listen, I'm gonna tell you something—"

"Now you're beginning to sound like that Miss Teal. Whatever happened to *simply divine* and *too, too lovely?* You better get your act together, Darlene, or better still, your head."

"Listen, I'm gonna . . . I don't need your advice and whether you're jealous or whether you're not, I don't need you to look after me."

"That's where your mother and you disagree."

"Oh her. We disagree all the time."

"Do you, Darlene? Looks to me like you're lost without her. Looks to me like she made you what you are, and now you don't know what to do with yourself." I yanked my winter coat out of the closet and put it on. Darlene was flopped on the edge of her bed trying not to notice. I got all the way to the door before she said, "Where do you think you're going?"

"Home," I said. "I know the way to the airport. You go through the graveyard and turn left." She failed to notice I didn't have my baggage with me. I turned around and saw she was stiff with fear. I won't say I enjoyed the sight. I won't say I didn't either.

"Don't," she said, and mumbled something more.

"What?"

"Stay. I don't . . . I don't think you'd stab me in the back. It was just something I said."

"Well, that's very little reason for staying, but thanks, for what it's worth."

"You're welcome," Darlene said in her little-girl voice.

chapter
nine

Since I already had my coat on, I said, "Come on, let's go out and see New York City. What with Miss Teal's poodle, we could be stuck in here the whole time."

"Oh we couldn't do that. She said we had to watch ourselves every minute. Besides I have to give myself a shampoo before tonight. And I . . . I could use a nap."

"Okay," I said, "you get a little beauty sleep. You never know when you might need it. And I'll just go out for a while and survey the territory."

"No, don't!" She started up. "You can't leave—I mean you might get lost." There's one unchanging thing about Darlene. Whoever she's being at the moment, you can see right through her.

"I didn't come to New York City to watch TV in the room and bicker with you, Darlene. And I won't get lost because I won't go far. Lock yourself in till I come back."

She sighed and looked pitiful. "Just don't be gone too long."

I got as far as the elevator when I heard her scream. As I said before, I have a very strong imagination for a farm girl. And the mental picture I got was of Rat Face, the bellboy, setting upon Darlene with criminal intent. I ran back, twisted the key in the lock, started right in and almost battered my brains out against the door. It only opened a crack because she'd put the chain on. "Darlene, are you all right?"

Confused *yuchs* of disgust from within. She yanked the door back. "Oh I could just throw up!" she said. "Look in the bathroom. I could just throw up!"

I went in there to see why. It was as nice a bathroom as you'd ever want to see. Pinkish marble everywhere and the faucets were all colored gold and shaped like fish. But it didn't take long to spot the trouble. There in the fancy sink was a tough old daddy cockroach. It was so big you could tell where it was looking. It was looking at me. And waving its feelers. I felt about half sick myself. I turned on the taps, but of course it was very citified and smart. It scampered up on the sink edge and dropped to the floor.

"Whoops, it got away."

Shrieks from the bedroom. "Verna, dooo something!" I jumped all over the floor trying to get that big devil. At last my shoe mashed him to roach heaven. You talk about a mess. I got it up with toilet paper and flushed the remains away. Then I strolled back in the other room.

Darlene was sitting in the middle of her bed with her knees drawn up. "Did you get it?" she said, wild-eyed.

"Never saw a thing. You must've been dreaming."

"Oh, Vernaaaa." I made my second exit, but not alone. Darlene and I set out together to see New York City.

It was one fancy hotel. They even played music for you in the elevator. Darlene was all for just exploring around in the lobby and not going outside. They had an indoor cafe with umbrellas over the tables, pretending to be outdoors. It was called Jardin de Paris, and there was a shop that sold nothing but satin and nylon lingerie and damask dinner napkins. In the window was some kind of a gown with a big feather boa at the neck. "Oh look," said Darlene, staring at it. "We have a hundred dollars apiece."

"Come on," I said. "You're getting to look enough like a kept woman as it is without that thing."

We turned in our key and stepped outside. There was a cutting wind and slush frozen in the gutters. But steam was rising out of the manholes in the street. It was a real vision of hell. We lingered there under the hotel porch wondering which way to go. Either direction we turned, the crowd was bound to knock us flat.

Darlene thought we ought to go back and ask them at the Paris cafe place if they made malteds. I stalked off down the street, though, and she had no choice but to follow.

We hadn't hit our stride before a middle-aged woman

stepped right up, in front of Darlene. She was an ordinary-looking woman except I happened to notice her shoes didn't match. That and the fact that she was hung all over with shopping bags. "Oh, sweetheart," she said right at Darlene, "you've got a face just like a rose and I'm a little short."

Darlene whimpered and shot behind me. So the woman shifted to me, "I say I'm a little short. All I need is forty cents more for the subway." I just kept walking, and the crowd swallowed her up.

"Verna, come on. Let's go back," Darlene whined. At the corner was a fellow with a big rack on rollers. On it was a sign and a big display of earrings for pierced ears. He had on a pair himself. The sign read ANY PAIR TWO DOLLARS OR MAKE ME AN OFFER. His rack was stuck in the slush, and he was struggling with it. Right next to him a policeman was writing him out a ticket. "Oh look," Darlene said, "only two dollars."

Never mind that she doesn't even have pierced ears, it was clear that Darlene's taste tended to wander off in all directions. But then I supposed her mother had been dressing her without training her to make her own decisions.

I started across an intersection. "Oh, Lord, not that way, Verna!" By then she'd taken to clinging to my arm. On the opposite sidewalk a whole show was going on, complete with music and dancing.

A big bunch of people—kids really—were bobbing up and down and chanting, with cymbals. They had their heads shaved except for a topknot, and there were white stripes painted on their scalps. All they were wearing were orange sheets and tennis shoes, regardless of the weather. They were singing or maybe praying, and it was the same sound over and over. With them was a girl in a long nightgown passing out literature. Even at a distance I figured she might be short forty cents for the subway too, so we turned to cross the other way.

I'd as soon have come to grips with the orange bedsheets as to dodge the traffic. It was one thing to keep out of their way and another to keep from getting covered with the black snow they were throwing up.

We fetched up on the far side, stained to the knees. "Oh don't you just hate this town?" Darlene said. "I just hate it, and I'm hungry." She'd long since taken to eating nothing but raw vegetables and cottage cheese at lunch. So she had to snack all the rest of the time to keep going. We went into a restaurant by the name of "Deli." The sign in the window said BREAKFAST ALL DAY.

We hunkered down on the only two seats available at the counter. "What's yours?" said the waitress, looking over her own shoulder away from us.

"I'll have a malted," Darlene said, "Chocolate and double—"

"We don't do malteds."

"What have you got?" I said.

The waitress sighed. "I got egg cream I got celery tonic I got—"

"Wait," I said. "Coke."

"Coke I got. Two? That's a pair. What else? Dollar minimum."

Somehow it was very important to try to keep this waitress calm. "Breakfast?" I said.

"Breakfast? It's afternoon," she growled. "Okay, breakfast. I got bagels I got lox I got omelettes any way but Western I got Danish but no prune or cinnamon I got toasted English I got—"

"Wait," I said, "scrambled eggs."

"With Cokes?"

"No, coffee."

"Make up your mind, Coke or cawfee."

"Coffee."

"And scrambled, right?"

"Right."

"That's a pair?"

"Of eggs?"

"No, of you. You both want the same thing? Look, I'm the only one on the counter I haven't got all day."

"Two of everything," I said quickly. She stamped off through a door with a sign on it that read THE COFFEE'S A QUARTER BUT THE SMILE IS FREE.

"Isn't she mean?" Darlene said. "I just hate her."

There were three girls sitting at the counter down from me. They were eating club sandwiches and smoking at the same time. I knew they were airline stewardesses because they all wore the same powder-blue uniforms. Anchored way up on their hair were those high round hats like extra heads.

The one next to me was telling a story to the other two: "I came home more dead than alive from Istanbul, and who do you suppose was in *my* bed?"

"Brenda and Leonard," said the next girl.

"Why yes. How did you know?"

"They'd been there day and night the whole time you were gone."

"So how did you handle it?" asked the third.

"What could I do? I was out of my mind with fatigue. I slept in the other bed."

"Just the three of you. Cozy."

"Oh very. And Leonard snores. He was in the bathroom the next morning for an hour and a half. What do you suppose men *do* in the bathroom all that time? So I says to Brenda, look, Brenda, your life's your own, but I pay my share of the rent *and* utilities and that entitles me to a good night's sleep and a *modicum* of privacy. And do you know what she has the nerve to say to me? She says she's getting a little tired living with the Virgin Mary. I tell you I went through the ceiling and I said to her. . . ."

My scrambled eggs were before me and cooling into a big yellow jelly while I eavesdropped on this tale. I couldn't take my ears off it. Darlene was tying into her breakfast and keeping one eye on the waitress in case she might decide to come back and bite off our heads.

The stewardesses stubbed out their cigarettes and hitched their long strap bags up on their shoulders. "Excuse me," I said to the story teller, "do you happen to know a girl named Sherri McDonald? She's a stewardess."

She whirled around, not having realized I was right there at her elbow, I guess.

"Does she fly with us?" she said, not sounding too unfriendly.

"Well, I don't know. I never thought to ask."

"We're Globe-Aire."

"Who'd she say?" asked one of the other girls.

"Sherri McDonald."

"Oh sure," said the third. "She's with us. I saw her in Curaçao day before yesterday."

"That's her," I said, feeling the world shrink up considerably.

"Oh, I know who you mean. Darling girl. Lives on Twenty-seventh Street. She'll always take the Indianapolis run."

"That's definitely Sherri," I said. Darlene was poking me by then.

"Is she a friend of yours?" said Brenda-and-Leonard's roommate.

"No, she's a friend of my brother."

"He wouldn't happen to live in Indianapolis, would he?"

"Close enough," I said.

"Well, that's one mystery solved. You really need an ulterior motive to bid for Indianapolis." They departed, flashing regulation smiles, but very pleasant. I was feeling pretty good about making a real human contact with New York.

"You shouldn't talk to strangers," Darlene hissed. "You never know."

When we came out of the Deli restaurant it was getting dark, and people were disappearing into holes in the ground. Our first engagement was no more than two hours off, so we made tracks back to the Regal Park Towers.

After a quick shower and change, I spent most of that time sitting on the foot of my bed. I was fully dressed in my all-purpose blue blazer and gray skirt with a dab of Miss Misty behind each ear and under my watchband. While Darlene gilded her lily in the bathroom, I watched the local news on the color TV. It was better than "Ironsides" and "Mod Squad" reruns combined.

First we had an on-the-scene conversation with an old-age pensioner who'd been mugged in his own kitchen. Then we had a daring daylight bank robbery with all the tellers lying on the floor and outlaws in ski masks backing out the door behind sawed-off shotguns. Then we had a drug addict being talked down off a fire escape with a whole audience of people watching from the alley. Then we had a short-circuit electrical fire on the subway line with people being given oxygen out of tanks. With this item was a man being interviewed who said he'd ridden the subways all his life, and he wanted to tell all of us watching on TV where we could stick the whole subway system as far as he was concerned. Then he told us.

The news ended up with a feature called "Twenty-four Hour Crime Clock"—two homicides, eighteen shootings, and twenty-nine nonfatal stabbings. This was considered low-average to light for a holiday season weekday.

I just sat there feeling privileged to be left alive. Darlene came out of the bathroom. She walked across to the bed to put some of her cosmetics into her evening bag. The sight made me catch my breath. She was so lovely it almost amounted to a religious experience. It didn't matter who she was or how she got that way. It didn't matter that 90 percent of her brain was back at Dunthorpe in her mother's head. It didn't matter that only a little while before she'd been clinging to my arm, helpless as a baby on the sidewalks of New York. She was perfect.

As she bent over her evening bag, her hair fell in a wave across her profile. A work of art. No, better than that. She was a beauty, instead of a beauty queen. And it was all because she thought she was alone. She wasn't striking poses or promoting seed corn or trying to cover up her emptiness. She was like the moon before there were astronauts.

Outside, the smoke and the clouds had lifted a little, and so the window framed her against the night-time city. She was part of it. Her dress was black—ten years too old for her, but just right. At her neck was a little circlet of rhinestones that were turning into diamonds.

She remembered I was there then, and the vision vanished. She gave me a look that was meant to wipe out any previous times she might have needed me. If I'd threatened to leave at that moment, she'd have handed me my suitcase.

There was a knock at the door. "Get it," she said.

The first person in the room was Miss Teal. She managed somehow to make the impression that she'd never left our sides. Behind her was the blondest man I ever saw. Never till then had I known there are men who dye their hair. And there was no question about this particular example. He had a deep, orangey tan, quite noticeable in the dead of winter. He was tall enough to look right over Miss Teal's head. And what he saw transfixed him.

While I'd been opening the door, Darlene had arranged herself with care. She was wearing very high-heeled black pumps. One pointed straight ahead of her. The other one, behind, pointed off to one side. It was the sort of balancing act that looks good in a fashion picture but a little studied in real life. She was inhaling, which made her look especially chesty. And a little smile played across her lips. The blond man summed her up in his first words, "Is that a Super Doll?" he said. "Is that ever an absolute dynamite Super Doll? Is that . . . a . . . dream . . . walking? I tell you frankly, she blows my mind. Really."

Miss Teal could hardly get him calmed down enough to make the introductions.

He tried to make up for missing me completely by giving me his business card.

Nobody'd ever given me a business card before, and I have it still.

BRUCE FENUCCI
Executive Vice President
INTERNATIONAL TALENT UNLIMITED AGENCY
models   theatricals   promos
commercials   industrial shows

He was trying to corner Darlene, but thought a little conversation with me was only right. "Well, Norma—"

"Her name's Verna," Miss Teal rasped. She was clearly his right-hand woman, and probably the brains of the outfit if they had any.

"Of course, Verna. You're . . . You're—"

"I'm along for the ride," I said.

"Oh no no no no no," blond, bronzed Bruce said. "We'll have to think up something more important as a function for you. You're—"

"Representing Super Doll," I said.

"Oh that's good. I like that. You pick up on things quick, don't you? She'll need an agent where she's heading!"

"She'll need more than that," I murmured. He was starting toward Darlene who was still frozen in place. Only the smile was melting.

"Just call me Bruce," Bruce boomed at her. "And how are things in Atlanta?" Darlene's eyes blurred.

"This is the Central United States Teen Super Doll," Miss Teal said to him. "Southern States is next week."

"Of course, of course. I can't keep track of all this

beauty pouring in from the great heartlands of America. Well, sweetheart, how do you like New York?"

"I just ha—love it," Darlene said and gulped. Bruce Fenucci had thrown an arm around her shoulders and was giving her the old squeeze. This caused the neckline on her dress to gap forward. He was peering down her cleavage. "Have we got a program lined up for you! Say, have we ever! Right, Teal?"

"The usual," Teal said in a tight voice, "beginning right now with the *boys,* Bruce."

"Oh yes," he said, "the boys. Come in, boys. You know the routine. Don't hang back."

The door was completely filled up by two of them. Real boys our own age, not middle-aged ones like Bruce. Obviously our escorts. I'd had four, maybe five dates in my life, none worth mentioning. And of course never any supplied by an agency. Though it's a blow to my pride to admit it, I think the agency did better by me than I'd done for myself. My gigolo was named David Winemiller. Darlene's was Skip something-or-other. I never caught his last name, and neither did she. David and Skip were classmates at a school called Van Cortlandt Academy.

Since David was stuck with me, I figured he'd lost the toss. I wondered if we were both in for a bleak time because of it. But he gave me a nice smile. And I tell you frankly if I'd had my pick, I'd have picked him.

The six of us went out to dinner at a place called Mama Minestrone's Italian Village, the noisiest place on earth.

The room was filled with big round tables of people yelling at each other. Ordinary small talk was out of the question. You either sat silent or screamed.

Across the table from me sat Darlene. Skip just stared at her from one side while Bruce talked continually at her from the other. There was something odd about him when you saw him in profile. His orangey tan stopped in a line just ahead of his ear. It looked an awful lot like make-up to me.

Darlene stared straight ahead at the bread sticks. David was between me and Miss Teal. I figured she could make herself heard anywhere so I naturally thought she'd occupy David's attention. But he kept turning my way.

"Did you have a good flight out?"

"I guess so. I don't have anything to compare it to. We didn't crash."

"What?"

"YES, A VERY GOOD FLIGHT."

"GOOD."

"Did you have a nice Christmas?" I asked him.

"A what?"

"A CHRISTMAS. DID YOU HAVE A NICE ONE?"

"Oh. Well—I had a nice Hanukkah."

It was a word I knew from someplace. I'd seen it in print. It was a sign in silver letters up among the Christmas decorations at the Deli restaurant: Happy Hanukkah.

"I'M JEWISH," David boomed. As luck would have it, there was a slight lull in the noise of the room.

A man looked up from the next table and said, "Who isn't?"

"Is that the Jewish Christmas?" I said straight into David's inner ear.

His nice big velvet eyes widened. "That's one way of putting it."

"Well, I mean, Christmas without the Christian part."

"But with the warmth left in," David said. We seemed to be hitting a wavelength of mutual hearing without bellowing so much.

"Do you mind if I ask you a personal question?" I said to him. "I've been wondering."

"If it's about religion, don't get too technical."

"It's not. Do they pay you to take us out?"

That got a laugh out of him. He shook his head. "We do it because Bruce lives down the hall from Skip's family. We're sort of slave labor with a free meal thrown in. By the way I recommend the cacciatore. It's the best thing they do here."

"You mean this is a regular thing with you two?"

"Let's see. So far it's been New England Super Doll and friend, Rocky Mountain Super Doll and friend, Gulf States and friend, and now we're up to Central United States and you. We've got a method worked out that keeps Skip and me both happy. Is it obvious?"

"I guess not. What is it?"

"Well, Skip is always the Super Doll's date. As good old Bruce would say, beauty blows his mind. But it also ties his tongue. Skip's a bit backward.

"He's met his match," I said. "And you?"

"Me, I always stick with Super Doll's friend. You meet a more interesting class of woman that way."

That dumfounded me. They brought us our cacciatore. It turned out to be chicken. Chickens follow me everywhere.

chapter

ten

Darlene peered up out of crumpled sheets. Without her eye make-up, she looked like a pale mole. "I don't think I can stand the pace," she mumbled, very invalidish.

"How do you know? You're not up yet." I was fully dressed before she stirred. I'd even had my first encounter of the day with a New Yorker. He was first cousin to the cockroach of the afternoon before. That sink was a regular roach rendezvous.

Darlene rose up halfway, "Oh I just *hated* him. All through dinner last night he had his hand up my dress. I just wanted to throw up!"

"Why sly old Skip. I heard tell he was backward."

"Who? Oh you mean that kid? I'm talking about Bruce Fennuci."

"Oh, well that's a horse of a different color," I said,

cracking myself up with my own early morning wit.

"Verna, you have the silliest sense of humor. I never know what you're laughing about. You're laughing on the inside sometimes too, aren't you?"

"Sometimes."

"That Bruce Fenucci. He's such an old . . . an old lecher."

"I thought you'd had experience handling older men." She was awake now, and I had only myself to blame for that.

"Just what's that supposed to mean?"

"Forget it, Darlene. When your voice gets all sophisticated-sounding, we end up scrapping. Get going or we'll be late."

"I repeat, what was that crack about older men?"

"It's none of my business, and I admit it. Now will you get dressed?"

"I know who you're making snide remarks about. A certain party who was at the homecoming dance with me. I saw you looking at us."

"All right," I said, "and just to show what a snide snoop I am, I noticed he was in your car at the airport too."

Darlene was slumped on the side of her bed, staring out at the clouds. "I got Mother to make him take me to the homecoming. He's Mother's property."

"I know that too, Darlene."

"Everything's Mother's. Everything in this whole stinky world belongs to *Mother*. You know where they are right this minute? I'll tell you where. He's all nestled up with Mother in that turquoise love nest of hers. She couldn't *wait* to get rid of me so she could. . . . God, do I hate turquoise!"

"Come on, Darlene, let's not get into anything."

"Look." She whipped around to face me. "You're along to keep me company, aren't you?"

"If you say so."

"I do say so. Then listen. Nobody listens to me. The best I can manage is to get people to *look* at me. That's right, isn't it?"

"Well, that's something."

"It's not enough. People look at Mother and they *listen* to her too. Everybody listens to her. Men, women, children, me, even *your* mother. And I haven't forgotten what you said to me yesterday either."

"Oh Lord, Darlene, what did I say?"

"You know good and well—that my mother made me what I am, and now I don't know what to do with myself."

"I take it all back."

"Don't bother. You were right."

The phone rang. "It'll be for me," Darlene said. It wasn't. She handed me the receiver and gave me a black look.

"Am I calling too early?" said the voice on the other end. "This is Sherri McDonald."

"You couldn't have called at a better time, Sherri, believe me." I got a shuddery feeling that maybe I was talking to my future sister-in-law. I wanted to say all the right things and make a good impression. I also wanted to keep the conversation going until Darlene disappeared into the bathroom. So I went into a long explanation about how Darlene had an appointment with a commercial photographer that morning. And how they were going to take a portfolio of pictures to publicize next summer's National Teen Super Doll Contest in Las Vegas, Nevada.

Oh I went on and on, but since I was talking mainly about Darlene, she just stood there listening. Finally I let Sherri get a few words in, and she invited me to come to her apartment for brunch.

"Yes, I'd like to," I said. "Darlene'll be busy this morning, so I'm free."

"No you're not either," Darlene butted in. "You've got to come with me."

I clamped my hand down over the mouthpiece and turned on her. "Darlene, since you resent your mother so much, don't expect me to take her place. I'm not going to be following you around the rest of your life, you know. You'll be on your own next summer at Las Vegas."

She stormed off, banging the bathroom door behind her.

Sherri and I had a complicated conversation about how to get to her place. I told her I might as well take a taxi cab since I had a hundred dollars. She said if I told that all over town, I wouldn't have it long. Somewhere in all this Miss Teal came rapping at the door and had to be let in. She was wearing a leopard-skin turban that made her look like a rabid cat.

She solved the problem by saying they'd drop me off on the way to the photographer. "And that'll take care of you for the morning," she added in her usual gruff but nothing-personal way.

Darlene finally reappeared only after Miss Teal threatened to come in after her. And just then the phone rang. Again it was for me, which was practically the last straw as far as Darlene was concerned. It was David. He offered to show me New York if I had nothing better to do in the afternoon. He also offered the information that this wasn't part of his obligation. I thought that was pretty nice, but when I turned to ask Miss Teal if I'd be free, she looked a little dubious.

"It's David," I said. "Not a stranger."

"Yeah, I unnerstand," Miss Teal said, clanking her bracelets uneasily. "That part's okay. I'm just thinking though. This afternoon they're going to interview Darlene. Maybe . . . you oughta be along."

"What kind of interview?" We were talking across Darlene again who was standing around looking pouty.

"Oh the usual," Miss Teal said. "They make a tape of all the Super Dolls' voices and get their opinions—establish their personalities sort of thing."

"Their opinions on what?"

"Current affairs, general interest topics, that bit."

I began to see the source of Miss Teal's worry. She

really did look troubled, but I said, "I don't see how I could help."

"You couldn't hurt either," she said darkly.

"You be there," Darlene yelled. "You be there, Verna, do you hear me?"

"I'll be there after I've seen David," I said, very quietly.

When we got to Sherri's address, I didn't want to get out of the cab. All I could see was a line of battered garbage cans. But Miss Teal assured me this was the place and edged me firmly out of the cab. They were already late. Darlene hadn't spoken all the way downtown.

When the yellow cab pulled away from the curb, it left the neighborhood a solid shade of gray. Sagging old stone buildings rose out of gray snow. There were drab little kids hanging around the parking meters giving me long, watery-eyed stares.

I climbed up the front steps feeling pretty sure that no airline stewardess lived there. There wasn't any glamour to it. But then what did I know? Everything so far had been just one surprise after another.

Whether Sherri lived there or not, I wished I hadn't come. I kept thinking about those stewardesses in the Deli restaurant. And of course I was remembering that Hal said Sherri was different. I was beginning to think I knew what he meant. And I didn't like the idea of being in the middle.

One of the row of buttons beside the front door was labeled McDonald, S. I rang, but nothing happened. The door made a funny buzzing noise, but nobody came to open it. I rang again. The door buzzed right back at me. It went on buzzing. I tried the knob and walked in.

I started down a long cabbage-smelling hallway. A huge lady with a mustache came out of a door. "I'm looking for Sherri McDonald."

"Top floor," she said and banged the door in my face.

After the third flight, I was winded, but a voice from above called down, "Keep climbing!" When I got to the fifth landing, Sherri McDonald was standing there at the top of the stairs.

Even in the half-light, I could see she was pretty. But she wasn't what I expected. For one thing, she wasn't wearing a uniform, so she looked like a civilian. She wasn't big and blonde and brisk either. She was rather small and dark, and she wore a sweater and skirt. And she was smiling, but it wasn't pasted on or painted over. It was nice and a little shy. It reminded me of the way Mama welcomes visitors.

I don't know what kind of pointless things we said for openers, though I meant to remember everything to tell later. The next thing I knew we were in the only room of her apartment. She gave me a goblet of orange juice while she busied herself around a little table set up for brunch.

"There I sleep," she said, pointing to the day bed I was sitting on, "and here I cook." She pointed to the other end of the room. "The tub's under the drainboard of the kitchen sink."

She lifted up a sheet-metal counter, and under it was

a strange rusty old bathtub up on claw feet. She watched my eyes widen. "This is sort of a warmed-over cold-water flat," she explained. "No real bathroom except in the kitchen, and the john's in the closet. It's pretty basic, but I'm not here very much."

Maybe not, but she'd done her best with it. It was like an oasis in the gray city. Bright-colored curtains added a little sunshine to the pale light outside. There were hanging baskets of asparagus fern and an avocado tree raised from a seed, all doing right well. An old-fashioned scrap quilt in the very pattern Grandma Henderson had made—double-wedding-ring—was nailed up on the wall like a tapestry. The floorboards, uneven as a barn loft, were waxed and smelling of lemon oil even through the cabbage aroma seeping in around the doorframe.

"I tried to paint the walls," she said, leaning over to pull something out of the oven, "but I kept getting a brush full of loose plaster." There were a lot of pictures hanging in unexpected places, covering up holes, no doubt. They were still lifes mostly, including the famous one of the sunflowers. And one was a piece of paper, framed. Just a few lines of a poem, carefully handlettered in colored inks.

I went over to read it while Sherri was pouring the coffee from the percolator into a china pot. The poem said:

> Music I heard with you was
> more than music,
> And bread I broke with you

> was more than bread;
> Now that I am without you,
>   all is desolate;
> All that was once so beautiful
>   is dead.

"Do you like poetry?" Sherri said. She was standing by the breakfast table, waiting until I'd read it.

"I like this one," I said. Mostly I was just being polite. I didn't know what I thought of it. I didn't know how it fitted in.

"So do I," she said. "There's something about it that's happy and sorrowful at the same time. And I guess it's the way I'd feel if . . . oh let's sit down, Verna. You must be starved."

When we faced each other across the table, I saw there were tiny perspiration beads on her upper lip, She was efficient and capable, but she was also a little flustered. I hadn't been the only one thinking about prospective in-laws.

Before us on the table was something golden and airy, puffed up over the sides of a pan. It was a soufflé, according to Sherri, and we were to eat it quick before it collapsed. She inserted a knife into the middle of it, saying that if the knife came out clean, the soufflé would be fit to eat.

It was delicious, even though it evaporated on the tongue almost before you could get a taste. Between us, we ate the whole thing, with a side order of toasted muffins. The jam was store bought, and I wished I'd thought to bring her a jar of homemade. I hadn't counted on her being the domestic type. I'd thought all steward- esses knew was to put thawed dinners on trays and carry them down the aisle. And I was crude enough to let that sentiment slip out in conversation.

She nodded, knowing all about the image. Then she told me of the time she'd delivered a baby in the middle of a flight over the ocean. She told it well too. My eyes were bugging out. Just how she'd had to get the mother stretched out on the floor and how she didn't cut the umbilical cord, but waited until they were on the ground and a doctor could be brought to the plane.

It made her job seem more meaningful. But she wasn't trying to make herself sound important. I liked her so much before we even mentioned Hal. I guess that was the best way to get acquainted. But then I realized she probably wanted to hear about him.

"Did you ever tell that story about the baby to Hal?"

"No, I didn't," she said, smiling a little.

"I think he ought to hear it. Might be useful to tell him next time you see him."

"Why?"

"Oh because he thinks your job's all glamour and exciting places and people, by which I think he means *men*. He doesn't tell me much. He's very cagey, you know. But I think he figures you're . . . you're going to slip through his fingers. He's scared to death, but if you tell him I said so, I'll be in trouble."

"We do have a communication problem," Sherri said,

smoothing the napkin in her lap. "And it's more complicated than that."

"He says you're different."

"He thinks I'm special because he loves me."

"Well, yes. But I think he means you're different from us. From us Hendersons, I mean."

"I wonder if I am," Sherri said. "I often wonder that. I feel as if I know you all. Of course, you're a surprise, Verna. Brothers always have trouble noticing their younger sisters are growing up, so he always makes you sound about twelve years old. But I know about your family. And about the farm. And about Aunt Eunice —your Aunt Eunice, I should say."

The mention of Aunt Eunice in the midst of this conversation brought me up short. Evidently Hal communicated better with Sherri than with the rest of us. "We're not such a bad bunch," I said. "And we manage to work around Aunt Eunice. You'd win her over in about five minutes. It'd be the longest five minutes of your life, but you'd manage."

I told her about how Aunt Eunice won the Miss Misty perfumes at the fair. And that reminded me of the old days when Hal had taken his prize heifer to show it. Sherri listened to it all, nodding to keep me going. Her eyes looked all starry. *This girl,* I told myself, *is madly in love with my brother.* That was obvious enough, but what surprised me was that I felt glad about it.

"I hope you two can work it out," I was fishing for information just like I have to do with Hal. But I really meant it, even if Sherri didn't want to confide in me.

"I hope so too," she said, fiddling with her coffee spoon. I decided to keep still for a while. "Did you know Hal wanted to be a doctor?" she said finally. I nodded. "And did you know he's given the idea up? Right now when he should be applying to medical schools, he's starting to go to job interviews—plain, routine jobs he isn't even interested in. It really does provoke me."

It was clear enough how my hardheaded brother's mind was working. He wanted to marry this girl before she got away. So he was junking his plans for all those years of medical school.

"I won't marry him if he doesn't go on to medical school," Sherri said. Her voice was quiet, but she was knotting up her napkin something fierce. "I'm going to tell him the next time I see him. And the time's running out."

Gloom descended. Though it was no time to be thinking of myself, I dreaded having to go home and face Hal, knowing this was in his future. "Isn't there any way to work this out?"

"Of course there is," Sherri said. "We could get married, and I'd go on working. Lots of girls work to help their husbands through school. I want to, Verna. I want to help him. I want us to do it together, but he thinks he has to carry the whole load. That's the real reason why my job's a threat to him."

"But you'd have to find another job."

"Why? Lots of stewardesses are married."

"I didn't know that," I said. "I thought they were all—"

"Swingers?"

"Well, yes. Sort of, I guess. Say, by the way, Sherri, do you happen to know Brenda and Leonard?"

"Oh heavens yes, everybody knows Brenda and Leonard," Sherri said absent-mindedly. Then she did a wonderful double take, "BRENDA AND LEONARD? How could you possibly know them?" She nearly vaulted over the table at me. I tell you I felt like a swinger myself—not in New York two days and already I knew all the dirt. Time enough later to tell her I'd been eavesdropping at the Deli restaurant. "You don't miss much, do you, Verna?" Sherri said, very baffled.

"People keep telling me that. Even old Bruce Fenucci noticed," I said wisely, and that just confused her more. It's nice to be able to impress your future sister-in-law. And that's just exactly what I decided Sherri McDonald was going to be, if I had any say in the matter.

"Listen, Sherri," I said, "let's see if we can't work up a plan."

chapter
eleven

*T*he bell rang, breaking into our girlish confidences. David stood in the doorway, right on schedule. He wore yellow construction boots and bleached Levis. But his upper half was pure Eastern prep school. A navy blazer with a crest and a long wool muffler wrapped around his neck with the tails falling in casual abandon. It was striped, no doubt in the Van Cortlandt Academy colors.

I made a mental note of this probably classy *ensemble* to convey to Ludmilla. I might just be able to awe her with an advanced peek at the Ivy League. Besides, maybe she'll meet up with him when they're all in the right colleges, the world being a small place once you get out in it.

It was nice too that Sherri saw I had a boy to show me the town. Is there a girl living who doesn't sometimes think she might end up as somebody's Aunt Eunice, even in these liberated days? If so, I haven't met her.

David said he wanted to take me to someplace called the Frick Collection. We were no sooner out of Sherri's building than he was at the curb playing King-of-the-Mountain on a snow heap, trying to hail a taxi. But I said, "Couldn't we take a subway instead? I've never been on one."

"You're not ready for that," David said.

"Oh but I am," I told him.

He skidded down off the snow hill. "Crazy country mouse," he muttered. We strode off down gray Twenty-seventh Street. And a little light snow filtered down, very white. At the Twenty-eighth Street subway station, which looked like a coal mine, I started through the turnstile before David could put a token in the box. The turnstile arm caught me just under the ribcage and nearly knocked the wind out of me. Then a train roared by and filled up both my eyes with grit. To think I'd passed up a cab for this.

The train that stopped for us was totally covered in spray-painted polka-dots as big as human heads. This is an illegal art form called graffiti, which David defined as "inner-city self-expression." Inside the car there were messages sprayed and grease-penciled everywhere—even over the windows. I couldn't make out most of them. You'd have to ride to the end of the line to read them all. Things like *Angel Luv Wilma* and *Red Hook Avengers Going Get Yor Ass*. I never saw anything like it.

We banged and rattled uptown, and everytime the train stopped I nearly fell off the slick plastic seat. Finally

David threw an arm around my shoulders to anchor me—at Fifty-first Street, as I recall. There are advantages to a poor sense of balance.

When we rumbled into the Hunter College–Sixty-eighth Street Station, David yelled, "Get out quick before the door catches you." I tell you, I ran for my life, only to realize that he was ambling nonchalantly out behind me. Country Mouse was being put on. I was, as Sherri would put it, provoked. But who could get mad at that engaging grin and those big, dark eyes? Not me.

The Frick Collection was right up by Central Park. It was like a palace, and as soon as we stepped in out of the cold, there was a sound of falling water. It was a free admission place, and we walked straight through the marble halls into a courtyard under a glass roof. There was a fountain in the center. The water fell into a pool where there were imitation frogs that spewed up water of their own.

The pool was edged with growing things–borders of real ivy and poinsettias, nothing plastic. There were even trees. It was like springtime in some far-off, *National Geographic* country.

We sat on a stone bench behind the pillars and watched the water fall. "I come here sometimes when I'm uptight about something," David said. "It's a big Rolaid for the emotions and Tums for the tensions."

It was a very soothing place, for a fact. Crammed with culture too, the sort of spot that would entrance Miss Castle. Chock full of *enriching and definite details.*

We walked on then, hand-in-hand, through the other rooms. There were great paintings of saints and sinners, pale women in white gowns and cattle in ponds, with names on them that had always been fuzzy at the back of my brain. Rembrandt, who painted himself, and El Greco and unpronounceables like Ingres and Velázquez.

David gave me a basic art course, but what I really liked best was that this museum had been somebody's house. There was furniture in it and beautiful carved shelves full of books and lamps made out of Chinese vases. The people who used to live there were Mr. and Mrs. Henry Clay Frick. His picture hung over the library fireplace. And he looked remarkably like Santa Claus in a business suit.

Beyond that was a very elaborate room with pictures painted directly on the walls by a fellow named Fragonard. Old-time ladies poised in flowered swings and gents in knee britches. And in corners too small for anything else, mischief-making cherubs peeped out. It might have been an overpowering room to linger in, but better by far than uninterrupted turquoise.

My favorite, though, was Mrs. Frick's own private sitting room. It was like lifting the lid on a little jewel box all lined in gray silk. Mrs. Frick's picture stood on her own personal writing desk. I don't suppose it's a great masterpiece, but she was a Victorian lady of true elegance with diamonds in her hair and piercing blue eyes. It was such a personal touch that I wanted to say hello to her and thanks for letting me in.

We circled through all the rooms and were back at our bench beside the pool. There, we fell to talking—real conversation this time, the kind you couldn't manage at Mama Minestrone's. David talked about going to something called a Montessori school when he was only three, which is a kind of school where you learn to do just as you please. And about being bar mitzvahed when he was thirteen and what that meant.

I told him my early history too—the Mount Yeomans grade school with its four teachers for eight grades. And about the long-ago winter we'd been snowed in for two weeks straight. And about being bused into Dunthorpe and what a major metropolis it had seemed to me at first—and until very lately, to be frank.

Thinking about home made me ask David what living all the time in New York was really like. I still couldn't imagine being so hemmed in all the time.

He thought for a while since nobody had ever asked him that. Then he said, "It's not the physical surroundings that matter. It's something else about New York, harder to put into words. It's like always being invited to a masquerade party and trying to decide whether you want to go or not."

That sounded pretty mysterious, so I waited while he unwound that big scarf from around his neck. "You can go down to the East Village on Saturday night and meet all the little Long Island weekenders playing the roll— you know, the windbreaker with the big sequined eagle on the back and the high boots, or whatever. And you

can move in the herd, buying grass in every other doorway and make the scene and blow your mind and play
out the whole stagy schtick. And you'll have plenty of
kinky company.

"Or you can forget about being with it, keep your
head together, have a few real friends and live a relatively
coherent existence. You always have the choice of faking
it in the hope it'll make you more interesting, or you
can settle for being yourself. And keep to a bare minimum of psychic status symbols. How's that for summing
up the Total Life Experience, including options?"

"Not bad at all," I said, "what I caught of it." What
I had caught of it sounded about like the way things are
anywhere. But I could see where New York offered you
more scope to pretend you were something you weren't.
That brought Darlene to both our minds, I guess, because
David said, "She doesn't know where she's heading, does
she—your friend, Darlene."

"No, she doesn't even know where she's been."

"Why do you care?"

Now there was a question I'd been waiting to ask
myself. "I don't think I know," I said. "My brother Hal
once had a heifer project. I guess Darlene's my lost lamb."

"That's too glib," David said. "You feel protective of
her as a human being." The irony in all this was that
we'd sat right past the time I'd promised to meet Darlene.
Somehow we'd consumed a couple of hours—closer to
three. We jumped up to leave. But we stopped at the
room where they sell postcards. I got enough to send to
everybody. Even the postcards there were pure class.

It's peculiar how partings give you a twinge—even from somebody you haven't even known a day. I said goodbye to David as soon as the cab drew up in front of the Park Avenue building where the agency was.

I thanked him for being nicer than he'd needed to be. And feeling a little awkward and sad, I started to slide out of the cab. He leaned over and kissed my cheek—just a quick brush. I was so surprised, I stopped sliding. He took my shoulders gently in both hands and kissed me again. A real one this time. "Come back again someday, Country Mouse, promise?"

"Promise," I said. Say what you will about New York cab drivers. That particular one waited very patiently through this farewell scene.

The next thing I remember clearly was Darlene sobbing her eyes out. The mascara was practically puddling. She was in a big executive suite on the thirty-third floor of a place called the Seagram's Building. When I caught sight of her, people were milling around, very nerve-wracked. They were bringing her glasses of water and rewinding a tape recorder. Miss Teal was jangling and barking. Bruce Fenucci was there too, with red veins standing out through his orange complexion. Darlene had definitely bombed.

"I don't know what you people *want* from me," she wailed, lifting her head up out of her hands. She caught sight of me. "Where the hell have you been?"

"She clutches up," Miss Teal said in her idea of a whisper. "All they wanted was to get an impression of her voice, a little natural conversation. But she came apart.

Drew a blank on everything except when we asked her opinion on the institution of the American family. Said she was the product of a broken home. From then on, it was all downhill. She did fine this morning at the photographer, but this afternoon—nothing. Zero.

"You oughta been here when we interviewed Miss Gulf States Teen Super Doll. Regular little fireball. She'd graduated from the Dixie Baton Twirling Academy and even did some twirls for us. She was good too—did a *tour jeté* and her own variations on the Double Pretzel and the Walk-Over. Darlene doesn't seem to have any hobbies, though."

"Talents, you mean," Darlene said, rearing up between us. "Why don't you just go ahead and give your precious Miss Baton Twirler the National Super Doll crown right now and forget about Las Vegas. You think I'm so damn stupid, but I can see this contest is nothing but a big fake. It's . . . it's *fixed!*"

"We don't judge the contest," Miss Teal said in a bored voice. We only handle the promotional angle. Frankly, we don't care who wins."

"Neither do I," said Darlene.

"Come on," Teal said. "Let's get her back to the hotel."

We stopped for an early, silent supper at the Jardin de Paris. But as quick as we got up to our room, Darlene disappeared into the bathroom where she sat soaking and sulking most of the evening. Miss Teal hung around for a while. "Nerves," she said to me while she paced around, none too calm herself. "Just nerves. Got kind of an inferiority complex too, doesn't she? No sweat, really, if she'll calm down. I mean this is no IQ contest. God forbid it should be.

"But look, you got to get her pulled together for tomorrow. That's crucial. It's her last commitment, but it's the big one."

I never seemed to absorb what was coming next in our schedule, so I had to ask her what was crucial about tomorrow. She said Darlene had to make a guest appearance on the TV panel show, "Spot the Frauds." Miss Teal acted like this shouldn't be news to me, but it was.

"Spot the Frauds" is this show where a panel of celebrities tries to figure out who's the real person and who the two fakers are. I must have seen it at home a hundred times. Darlene was to be the real regional Teen Super Doll of course. And there'd be two other girls there with her, just pretending to be Super Dolls. The panelists ask them questions and then vote on who they think the real one is.

"Considering the way she dissolved today, I dread to think how she'll be in front of that panel of sharpies. There's a studio audience too," Miss Teal muttered as she stalked around. "I wish we'd scheduled this with the Gulf States girl instead. You know, the baton twirler. There's a gal who could carry it off."

She left finally. Her poodle was way overdue for his walk and subject to accidents. At the door she issued a dire warning to have Darlene ready by 8:00 A.M. because you can't keep a TV show waiting. It has something to do with the cameramen's union.

To while away the rest of the evening, I arranged all my Frick postcards on the desk top. It didn't matter that I'd be home before they got there. This was my first chance to send mail from anyplace, and I wasn't going to pass it up.

It was a shame to part with them, and I finally decided to keep the one of the fountain in the courtyard for myself. But I addressed the rest to my nearest and dearest. Pretty soon, Darlene wandered out. She was in her bathrobe with a hotel towel wrapped around her head. Her face was scrubbed pale. She looked like a waterlogged nun. I had the feeling she'd taken on one of her alien personalities, and it made me uneasy.

She started over toward her bed though, like I was the Invisible Woman. I don't like a scene, but then I don't like being ignored either. "Nice evening," I remarked, to get a rise out of her.

"What are you doing?"

"Writing some postcards."

"What are they of?"

"Come and see." I knew she didn't want to act interested, but she came over anyway, balancing that towel on her head. She glanced down over my shoulder.

"What was it, some kind of museum?" I nodded. "That kid take you there today?"

"Yes. David took me. I've written cards to the girls. Do you want to sign them too?"

"Why should I?"

"Why shouldn't you? They're your friends too, if you want them to be."

"I didn't get to see that museum or whatever it is. I didn't get to see anything. *You* had a nice day, didn't you? You went to see that girlfriend of your brother's and then that kid—"

"David."

"David took you out, and you had a real nice day."

"Yes, I did. I'm sorry I was late and didn't make it to your—interview."

"It doesn't matter," Darlene said. "It was up to me to sink or swim. I'd have sunk anyway." That made me look up at her in some surprise. It was a very sensible remark. She settled in the easy chair and stuck her legs out very uncharmingly. I still sensed a change in her. She was softer. "Tell me what you did today," she said.

"I already have."

"No, I mean everything. What your brother's girl is like and that kind of stuff. And, you know, where you went and all."

So I did. I told her about the bathtub in Sherri's kitchen and what a soufflé is. And since she still seemed attentive, I told her about how Sherri's job is a threat to Hal, not really because he thinks it's glamorous, but because he thinks it's wrong for a wife to support her husband, even in a good cause. I didn't mind telling her all this, but I couldn't quite believe she was interested.

She didn't get up till I'd run down though. I'd talked

practically through all the pictures in Mr. Frick's house. I stopped short of the double kiss from David however. I don't tell everything.

She went over and sat down on her bed. I knew she'd listened to the limit of her attention span, probably beyond. She began talking. It was about herself, but this time it amounted to something. "You know the first thing I can ever remember in my whole life?" she said. "It was watching the Miss America Pageant at Atlantic City on TV. The first song I ever learned was 'Here She Comes, Miss America.' While other kids were learning nursery rhymes, I was learning 'Here She Comes, Miss America.'

"You want to know something? When Bert Parks started singing, my mother would sing along with him, only she'd sing, 'Here She Comes, Darlene Hoffmeister.' It sounded awful that way, but I never could stop Mother. Nobody can. We watched that pageant every year—together. Finally, I got so I wouldn't miss it.

"Verna," she said, almost in a whisper, "I never had a chance."

chapter
twelve

*I*f you don't count the Fricks' house, the prettiest place in New York is Rockefeller Center. Being New York, they'd have to have the biggest Christmas tree in captivity. And there it was, all its decorations tinkling in the breeze. Below it there's a skating rink.

Even at 8:25 in the morning, the skaters were out. Girls in flippy little fitted costumes and body stockings. Boys with lean, athletic hips and big shaggy ski sweaters. Fat, gray-haired people just as graceful as the young skinny ones. Even couples skating face-to-face like ballroom dancers. There was music piped in too. Cold as it was, I wished I could stand there watching them all day. I was soon to wish it far, far more.

Miss Teal hustled Darlene and me into the building and up in a private elevator that let us off backstage in a television studio. If you've ever wondered what goes on behind the scenes in TV land, I'll tell you—chaos.

Cables snaked all over the floor, and people darted in every direction. A girl with a clipboard like a gym teacher rushed up to us. "You're Miss Teal for the Super Doll sequence, right?"

"Right."

"We're in trouble," the girl said, tossing back her unruly hair. "Big trouble. One of the Super Doll frauds is a no-show. Got flu and can't make it. She was fully rehearsed and everything."

Miss Teal sighed, and I think it was from relief. She was ready to lead Darlene speedily away. But the girl with the tossing mane said they had a "time slot to fill" and it would have to be filled. They already had the other impersonator, but she wasn't particularly strong since she was somebody's twenty-two-year-old secretary and not very convincing Super Doll material.

Can you see it coming? I couldn't for a minute. But then they were looking at me. "Oh, no," I said and meant it. "Not me. I can't do it. Not on TV. That's ridiculous. Absolutely not." Darlene was giving me the strangest look—and Teal already had me by the upper arm.

Icy fingers clutched my heart, as the saying goes. Then I was being led away through the dim backstage light to the other side where a bunch of people were gathered, drinking coffee. The girl with the clipboard led the way down a flight of steps and through a doorway. Over it was a sign that read TALENT ONLY. Teal never turned me loose until we were in a room full of dressing tables and three-way mirrors.

There sat the other Super Doll faker—the twenty-two-year-old secretary. She did look a little bit long in the tooth for a teen-age beauty queen. But there were a couple of make-up men working her over, removing five or so years of wear and tear from her face. She was starting to look like a doll, if not exactly a Super Doll. I still wasn't accepting the fact that this could have anything to do with me. But my heart was going like a kettledrum.

"Okay," said Clipboard, "you two, start taking off your clothes."

Being a veteran of fashion shows, contests, commercials, and other stagy schticks (notice my new David vocabulary), Darlene shrugged her coat off and stepped out of her skirt.

While I was fumbling with myself, I ripped the middle button off my jacket. "Take it easy," Teal said out of the corner of her mouth. We stood there for long moments in our slips, and neither Darlene nor I spoke. The radiators were blasting away, but my teeth were chattering.

Somebody stepped up behind me and threw a big plastic bib over my head, noose fashion. Then I was sitting in front of a dressing-table mirror. Hands were working me over—two pairs. One pair busied themselves in my hair. The other was rubbing something creamy into my face. I was beginning to disappear before my very eyes. The mirror fogged up with hair spray. For some peculiar reason, it was the same as being in the dentist's chair. I had a crazy vision of poor Bernice at the mercy of her orthodontist.

The clipboard girl stepped up to my side. "Okay now, we have to be quick. I got just five minutes to work you up. Now listen, what's your name?"

"Verna Henderson."

"Wrong. Your name is Darlene Hoffmeister."

"Oh."

"Say it."

"My name is Darlene Hoffmeister."

"Okay. When you get on the stage, say it like you mean it. You'll be in the number three position. What honor have you received?"

"I . . . I don't think I can do this," I said in a plaintive voice.

"YOU . . . ARE . . . GOING . . . TO . . . DO . . . IT!" Clipboard said. She sounded really vicious, but then this girl's job depends on "filling time slots."

"I'm Teen—"

"Wrong. Try again."

"I'm Central United States Teen Super Doll." (Oh good grief.)

"Right."

"Where were you crowned?"

"St. Louis. Now wait a minute. Are these the questions the panel will ask?"

"Oh no, you've got to be ready for anything. How many girls did you compete against?"

"I don't know," I said. "I wasn't there."

"Look, fake it. This is *acting.* Say something convincing."

"Thirty girls," I blurted. Somebody with a bristly brush was yanking my hair out by the roots. Between that and the third degree, I was being dismembered, body and soul.

"If you are crowned National Teen Super Doll, what will your responsibilities entail?" The questions kept coming. My mind tried to leap nimbly ahead of them.

"I will make public appearances across the United States, representing American youth."

"Good, now you're in the rhythm of it. Keep it flowing. Will you be chaperoned?"

"Yes," I said, quite confidently, "my mother will accompany me." Weirdly enough, when I said that, I thought of Darlene's mother, not my own. I really could feel my own identity ebbing away. *Is there a life after death?* came a lunatic voice inside me. *Yes, and if you're not careful, you could come back as Darlene!* I began to quake with hysterical laughter.

"Knock it off," a voice said. "I'm trying to put on your mouth."

"You'll do fine," the clipboard girl said. "Sign this in two places." She thrust a document onto the dressing table. Some of the pore-filler or whatever it was had slopped over my lower eyelids. I could hardly see. "It's just the standard contract for the show. You'll get fifty dollars for every panelist who votes for you. If nobody guesses the real Super Doll, the three of you split five hundred dollars."

Fat chance, I thought, though I didn't say it since my

mouth wasn't finished yet. I'd have gladly paid *them* to let me off.

Hands whipped off my plastic bib and pressed something spiky down on my head. I blinked the creamy stuff out of my eyes. The mirror cleared. I was looking at myself. It was me again, but somehow changed. My hair, for so long trained arrow-straight, was flipped up at the ends and just grazed my shoulders. The curled part was stiff with hair spray, but I liked the look. I reached up to it, but a voice behind me said, "Hands off!"

My face should have been a mask since it was well layered over. But the make-up boys were true artists. It looked like my real skin, lips, eyebrows . . . but better. And on top of all this, a crown glittering in rhinestones. Beverly Fenster should see me now!

I grinned without shattering my new brushed-on mouth. The Super Doll in the mirror grinned back—and said, *You big fraud.* There I sat having the time of my life. Then I remembered what this was all for.

"On your feet," came a new voice. Two wardrobe women were holding up a long white dress. It was a formal, but it looked like something sacrificial virgins wear when they're being thrown into volcanoes. It went over my head without touching the artwork on my hair and face. I couldn't tell whether it was a good fit or not, never having had on a long dress.

But the wardrobe women were experts too. They pinned up the back until the dress fitted just right. In fact, better than right. I seemed to have more figure than usual. To think I'd been hiding my light under a bushel of denim and Hal's old lumberjack shirt. The final touch was a blue satin ribbon that ran from shoulder to hip with big gold letters on it: "Super Doll."

"What's your name, kid?" one of the wardrobe women said casually.

"Darlene," I said to her, "Darlene Hoffmeister."

"For real?"

"No," I said, "Just for now."

She led me over to a three-way mirror so I could get the full effect. But when I stepped up to it, I could see over my own shoulder my fellow fraud on one side of the room and Darlene on the other. Impersonator number one was smoking a cigarette and looking like she wished she was back at her typewriter. Darlene had just been slipped into her dress, which she filled out more than adequately without being pinned. I caught her eye in the mirror, but not her mood.

They gathered us all together, and the clipboard girl reappeared. "Not bad at all, considering," she said.

"There's no time for a rehearsal. You're going to have to run this through cold." I was suddenly freezing again. They herded us up the stairs. For the first time in my life, I had to gather up my skirts. I felt like Martha Washington.

The minute we arrived backstage, everybody turned to look at us. There were other threesomes waiting to go on too. A famous pro football star and two likely imposters in shoulder pads. A lady being trained in the astronaut program and two fakers, all suited up in silvery astrogear. It was like an especially spooky costume party. Everybody else was drinking coffee around a big urn, but we weren't allowed any for fear we'd spill it down our white dresses. I moved over next to Darlene. "Do you mind?" I said to her.

"Mind what?"

"That they're having me do this. I guess I could have refused."

"Why should I mind?" she said in her hardest voice. But then she reached out and took my hand. I nearly jumped. Her hand was colder than mine. "No," she whispered, "I'm glad. I'm tired of . . . of being alone all the time." She squeezed my hand hard and let it drop. Then she turned away, icy and withdrawn, and perfect.

I'd never stood in the wings of a stage before, and I'll tell you right now I don't care if I never do again. The stage was divided into daylight and dark. We stood in the twilight to one side and a glare of light from the front flooded back, reflecting on the lady astronauts' uniforms and picking up the gold letters on our sashes. There was a sudden burst of applause. I nearly went through the floor. There was an entire theater full of people out there. I thought of the dumb old joke about the Roman basketball game: Lions 90, Christians 0.

"Good! One more time!" came a voice, followed by another burst of applause.

"Has it started?" I asked Miss Teal, who was lurking in the shadows with us.

"No," she said. "They're just warming up the audience. They have to practice their clapping. It won't be long now. You're up first." The clipboard girl raced across backstage and hustled us all into a far corner. The celebrity panelists were arriving from the stage door and weren't to catch a glimpse of us ahead of time. I shrank back but caught a sight of them. They were wandering in, chatting. Just another day's work for them, I thought, and my mind boggled. How many times I'd seen them on the old tube, and there they were, in the flesh. My flesh was crawling.

There was another burst of applause, this time spontaneous. The master of ceremonies of "Spot the Frauds" had just walked on—Bert Hartley, the housewives' heart-throb. He began to greet the panelists, making their entrances from the far side.

The crowd roared. Miss Diana Renfrew—international singing star and veteran panelist (thunderous clapping). Mr. Larry Grissom—durable Broadway leading man (whoops of recognition). Miss Penelope Chase—hilarious comedienne (screams of laughter at the sight of her). Mr. Sam Ryan (movie critic and man-about-town). The applause swelled and dropped away, replaced by a filmed commercial for panty girdles.

"Super Dolls up first. Get 'em on their marks." Somebody led us to the middle of the stage. There were three big X's painted on the floor. The other impersonator was maneuvered right onto the first X. Darlene and I fell in on ours. My nose was an inch from the partition separating us from—fourteen million viewers. "Gosh, I wish I was home," I said to the partition. It parted.

Canned music, the familiar theme song, blared. At first, I was struck blind. Dazzling lights hit us from every angle. The cameras were only one-eyed shapes. "SUPER DOLL NUMBER ONE! WHAT IS YOUR NAME PLEASE?" boomed Bert Hartley.

"My name is Darlene Hoffmeister," the secretary said. The real Darlene next to me quivered.

NUMBER TWO, WHAT IS *YOUR* NAME PLEASE?"

"My name is Darlene Hoffmeister," Darlene said, tonelessly.

"NUMBER THREE, WHAT IS *YOUR* NAME PLEASE?" I was sure that under pressure I'd say my real name. Either that or have a terminal attack of laryngitis.

"My name is Darlene Hoffmeister." As soon as I'd said it, I realized that was the only easy part.

Host Bert Hartley began to read an affidavit, which he told the panel to follow on copies at their desks. My vision was clearing. Out of the corner of my eye I could see Miss Penelope Chase, the comedienne, slipping on her glasses. She looked very businesslike. *"I Darlene Hoffmeister,"* the master of ceremonies read, *"was crowned Central United States Teen Super Doll . . ."* Mr. Larry Grissom, the Broadway actor, was hitched back in his chair, not looking interested. *"to be held next summer in Las . . ."* Mr. Sam Ryan, the movie critic, was scanning us carefully. It seemed to me his eyes were lingering on

Darlene, but I couldn't be sure. *"Vegas, Nevada. Similar regional competitions have been held through the country to select . . ."* My knees were locked. We were to walk over and sit down at desks, facing the panel. I had to lead off, and I knew I couldn't. I was rooted to the floor. Stagehands would have to come on and carry me off like a fence post. This was one time the show wouldn't go on. "Strike the set!" my kneecaps screamed.

But Bert stopped talking, and the music began again. I was walking—toward the seat. I caught my first glimpse of the audience, row on row of them. The crown was digging into my head. "TO START OUR QUESTIONING, LET'S BEGIN WITH MISS DIANA RENFREW. TAKE IT AWAY, DIANA!"

"Thank you, Bert. Super Doll Number . . ." What was my number? Either one or three. Which? Three. That was it. Three. "One. How old are you?" The twenty-two-year-old secretary said she was fifteen, causing the panel to make little notes on their pads.

"Super Doll Number Two, how did you happen to enter the contest?"

Silence from Darlene. Bert Hartley had to point at her. "What?" Darlene said. Miss Renfrew repeated the question, but faster.

"Oh, I . . . my mother made me do it." This got a howl of laughter out of the audience. I remembered that time in Miss Castle's class when everybody had turned on her. Don't do that to her. Don't.

"Number Three," Diana Renfrew said . . . the buzzer

cut her off. They moved on to Mr. Larry Grissom, who had the whitest teeth I've ever seen, the better to eat you up with, my dear.

"Number Three," he said, "Have you previously competed in similar contests?"

"No," I said into the microphone, "I'm . . . rather new at this." The questions came faster. I seemed to manage an answer without knowing what I was doing. But lacking a script, Darlene was a goner. Miss Penelope Chase nailed her. "Super Doll Number Two, what useful purpose do you think beauty contests serve?"

"Well, they . . . well, I don't know. I guess they . . . I don't know."

"Thank you," Miss Chase said, marking her pad. "Number Three, I understand one of the awards for the national winner is a full-tuition scholarship. If you win, what do you plan to study in college?"

What a time to be confronted by your future. I had to say something fast, and confidently. "I plan to study human psychology," I heard myself replying.

"Oh," said Miss Chase. "Why?" (Why doesn't this woman lay off me and move on to the others?)

"Because I've been gathering a lot of material on the subject lately that I'd like to sort out later." I knew I was babbling, and my white gown was sopping from armpit to waist.

"Interesting," said Miss Chase. Number One—" The buzzer caught her. Time must have been running out as Mr. Sam Ryan began. Either that or my head was whirling. He zeroed in on Super Doll Number One, who was a mumbler. Then he asked Darlene where she came from, and she had difficulty remembering Dunthorpe. The audience rippled with giggles. Just as he shifted to me, the final buzzer rang.

"And now, panelists, your difficult task is to determine the REAL Darlene Hoffmeister, Central United States Teen Super Doll. IS IT NUMBER ONE? OR IS IT NUMBER TWO? OR COULD IT BE NUMBER THREE? MARK YOUR BALLOTS PLEASE!"

There was another commercial break then. We were all wilting under those terrible lights. Another minute of this, and my entire face would melt and run down my bosom. "LET'S START THE VOTING WITH MISS DIANA RENFREW," Bert Hartley said.

"Well, Bert," Diana said, lifting up her ballot, "they were all excellent, but I wasn't convinced that Number One is a fifteen-year-old girl. Number Two is quite a beauty, but I'll cast my vote for Number Three. She strikes me as the kind of girl who would be chosen to represent young people."

Good grief, I got a vote. It was Larry Grissom's turn next. "I may be wrong," he said, not sounding as if he much cared if he was, "but I agree with Diana. I was tempted to vote for Number Two, but I think she's just a well-chosen—and well-endowed—imposter. Number Three strikes me as the genuine article. That's just my gut reaction." He tossed his pencil down.

Miss Penelope Chase was inclined to agree, saying that

even beauty contest winners these days are expected to have brains. I thought that was rather rude and hoped Darlene wasn't listening.

Mr. Sam Ryan voted for me too, by the process of elimination, he said, which could have meant anything. The audience stirred, realizing I'd gotten all the votes before I did. Me, the All-American Faker. I only truly comprehended it when Bert Hartley asked the real Darlene Hoffmeister TO STAND UP PLEASE!

Every one of the panelists was looking at me. Their eyes jumped away when Darlene stood. I made myself look up at her. She was smiling brightly. Maybe she was relieved it was over. Or maybe she was planning what she was going to do to me.

I had time to think how she and I had come close to an understanding over the past few hours. How we'd talked the night before. Not a real conversation maybe, but each of us had listened to the other. I supposed all that had been wiped out by this idiotic television show. It was like I'd robbed Darlene of the only thing she had. Or as she'd say, stabbed her in the back. If I felt any pride in being mistaken for a teen-aged sex symbol or whatever, it was well buried under the thought of what this might do to Darlene. I guess I always had felt protective of her, like David said. Maybe because it was the only way to relate to her at all.

chapter
thirteen

*W*e had lunch that day looking straight down on the steeples of St. Patrick's Cathedral. It was a very grand restaurant at the top of an office building— almost my old dream of a penthouse come true.

But I appreciated the thick window glass more than anything else since I was reasonably sure Darlene would fling me off a convenient roof if she had the chance.

Lunch though it was, it felt like the Last Supper. Darlene hadn't opened her mouth since we walked off that stage. And though I wouldn't have believed it, Miss Teal was clearly embarrassed. Even her bark sounded uncertain. "Order anything you like, girls . . . Sky's the . . . ah . . . limit." The sky was right outside the window, and it looked to me like a storm was brewing. Miss Teal kept getting her bracelets tangled up in the silverwear. Knives and forks hit the floor continually.

When Darlene finally spoke, it was to the waiter. And

to my amazement, she ordered practically everything on the menu. Whatever happened to cottage cheese and carrot sticks? In sheer confusion, I ordered the Weight Watcher's Special and banana cream pie. Miss Teal hemmed and hawed over her menu so long the waiter nearly took it away from her.

Silence fell again, broken only by Miss Teal saying there'd just be time for some shopping before we had to leave for the airport. She was sure we'd like to take some souvenirs back home . . . or something. . . . Her voice trailed off.

The service in that place must have been especially slow. Finally, I couldn't take it any longer and made for the powder room. I stayed in there as long as I dared, toning down my TV make-up with Kleenex and washing my hands till the fingertips were ten white prunes. Then I stared at the flocked wallpaper until my eyes danced.

On the way out, I spotted a phone booth and called Sherri. I told her the curious turn events had taken that morning. I even read off to her what it said on my "Spot the Fraud's" check. It was for $166.65—my cut of the $500 for skunking the panel. I was a rich woman, but the check seemed about as fake as the experience. Then Sherri and I outlined our future plans again. While we talked, Darlene flitted by toward the powder room.

She wasn't in there long. Probably she timed herself according to my phone call. I'd no sooner hung up than Darlene and I were face-to-face in the dim hallway. For all I understood about her, we kept coming to these moments when I felt intimidated. Moments I just wanted to get through with neither of us getting hurt.

She took a half step toward me. "Look," she said, "I'm not mad. It's just . . . I'm quiet because I'm trying to think. I have things to think about. But I'm not mad. Okay?"

"Okay," I said, and smiled at her just because she was looking so sober. Like a little girl in a sandbox. We started back to the restaurant, but she had another surprise in store. She turned and said, "When we go shopping, why don't you get a can of hair spray?"

"A what?"

"Some hair spray. Keep your hair like that, flipped up at the ends. It's right for you." Then she strode off through the tables. All the men in the place stopped chewing to watch her pass. But she sailed through them all like Moses parting the Red Sea. I don't know if she noticed them or not.

At home there was an invitation to Bernice's New Year's Eve party waiting. And so I had no more than a couple of days to recover from New York. Not that I ever plan a complete recovery.

Glad as I was to see home again, I talked myself hoarse about that trip. I was talking whether anybody was listening or not. Aunt Eunice listened her share, though she felt that such experiences as I'd had probably did permanent damage to anybody fool enough to take part in them. I brought her a silk scarf made in Italy with fringed edges and her initial. It came from Saks Fifth Avenue store. She said it was the most extravagant-looking thing she'd set eyes on yet, and where would you wear a thing like that? Then she reached over and patted the back of my hand.

Later, she told Mama to tell me it was the loveliest thing she had and wait till they see her wearing it at church.

I brought Mama a fancy French contraption made out of welded wire to hold eggs in. It was meant as a kitchen utensil, but it was pretty enough to use as a dining-room centerpiece, even with eggs. "Well I never," she said. "What'll they come up with next?"

Mama thought it was a doggone shame that the Dunthorpe television channel didn't carry "Spot the Frauds." She wanted to see me in my glory—and Darlene too, she added. Never mind, Mama," I said. "I wouldn't mind the fame, except I'd hate to pay the price of it." I was remembering something Moon had said once about the reactions to Darlene's climb to stardom. But I was thinking more about Darlene and me.

I didn't really figure she thought I'd plotted to show her up on that TV show. But having everybody in town— her mother included—seeing it could be another matter. It'd probably end up as another anonymous poem in the school newspaper. Some experiences don't improve with repeating.

Still, Mama had me acting out the whole program in the middle of the kitchen—twice. Hal happened in the back door and caught my second show.

He pushed his cap onto the back of his head and stood there grinning. Then he said, "I told you your day was coming." Mama didn't know what he was talking about. But I remembered that summer afternoon on the top of the double Ferris wheel.

Mama and I made a special, hurry-up trip in to Dunthorpe and bought a length of dark green velvet. We whipped it up into a long skirt for me to wear to Bernice's party. I figured that since I'd walked across a stage before fourteen million people in a long dress, I could make it up the Ransoms' porch in one. I got a pair of high-heeled sandals that were mostly narrow straps to go with it. In New York I'd bought the top for this outfit—an ivory-colored satin blouse. Listen, you can spend a hundred dollars at Saks Fifth Avenue without losing sight of the front door.

The major part of my plan was to get Hal to take me to the party. And since I was nervous about pulling that off, I let Mama in on the whole scheme. When I outlined the particulars to her, her eyes got big as silver dollars. Then they filled up with tears.

I had to call Bernice too and work things out at her end. She'd just gotten my postcard showing the Fricks' house and had to know all. I told her everything and bragged a little about David. But I left out the part about the TV show. I was on that phone for an hour, and Dad, who rarely comments on such things, did mention something about message units.

On New Year's Eve day I was more keyed up than

even New York could make me. It was one of those hard-frozen, snowless days. My first step was to get Hal to myself. He and Dad were doing some carpentry out in the cob house, which complicated matters. As soon as lunch was over, I caught up with Hal on the back porch. He and Dad were heading back to work. And when I told him I wanted the two of us to drive out to the reservoir, he thought I'd taken leave of my senses.

"Verna, do you know it's the middle of the winter?" he said in that big-brother tone of voice. "What are we going to do out there? Break the ice and swim?"

"Who knows where you'll be next summer," I said, as pathetic as possible. "Maybe it's. . . ." I let my voice trail off on purpose. It was one of my better performances, not counting TV.

"Hey, where's my carpenter's helper?" Dad called from the yard. But Mama stepped out of the back door and shook her head at him just once. He shrugged and disappeared around the corner of the cob house, which is where he goes anyway when things get complicated.

The truck bounced hard on the frozen ruts out toward Persimmon Woods. The heater was on the blink too. I had on a muffler and a stocking cap and mittens. Whatever glamour I could manage, I was saving up for evening. Above his gloves, Hal's wrists were turning blue. We didn't say much. He was a little put out with me anyway. I'd reported on my visit with Sherri, but I'd kept my account to a bare minimum. And he was too proud to pump me for details. The only reason I'd got him off on this wild goose chase was that he thought I might talk some more about my visit to Twenty-seventh Street. He was so lonesome for her he could hardly stand it, as any fool could see.

With the leaves off the trees, we could see the reservoir from the gate. It showed up suddenly, with the wind whipping little cyclones of frost off the ice. On the last stretch of the lane the truck pitched around so bad that Hal finally swerved off and drove overland right down to the shore. He killed the engine and started smacking his hands together.

Now that I had him where I wanted him, I didn't know how to begin. I wanted to get everything said before we froze to death. The windshield clouded up from our breath. All around us was an unearthly quiet, and that gave me an idea. "I wonder if you could hear the church bells on a day like today," I mused.

Hal gave me a strange look, but then he was remembering. "Good old—what was it?—Weavers Rest," he said. "Have we come out here to see if the steeple's sticking up out of the ice?"

"Let's get out and look," I said. Along the edge of the reservoir brown water bubbled up at the edge of the ice crust. We puffed along, crunching the brittle weeds under foot. I climbed on a rock big enough for two and stood up there braving the elements. Hal scrambled up beside me, and before he got his breath I was ready for him. "I don't know how Dad could have done it alone," I said.

"*Now* what are you talking about?"

"I'm talking about Mama and Dad and how they've worked hand-in-glove together all these years." I was looking over to the far shore, but I knew I had his attention. "Everything they've ever done, they've done together. Hard times at first, I guess, though they never mention it."

"I guess so."

"Worked for everything they got."

"Dad's a good farmer."

"Hal, they're both good farmers."

The wind cut our eyes, but neither of us moved. He knew by then I hadn't led him out here to no purpose. "What are you saying, Verna?"

"I'm saying I know a girl in New York City who wants to be with you and work alongside you and . . . and everything just like Mama and Dad have done."

"It's not the same, Verna. Times are different—"

"People aren't—"

"Everything's different. Do you realize I'd be pushing thirty before I got through medical school and internship and the rest of it? You don't ask a girl to wait six or seven years."

"No," I said, nudging some little pebbles off the big rock, "you don't ask a girl to wait—not a girl who wants to share it with you and help. Not a girl like Sherri."

"Look, I'm willing to give up . . . to get a job so I can give her—"

"You'll lose her that way, Hal. You'll lose her by trying to give up and give instead of sharing."

It got quiet on our rock then, very quiet. My toes were numb, but I was standing my ground. "Did she tell you that?"

"I don't carry tales," I said, though actually I've been known to.

"Well, I can't," he said. "I can't lose her."

"It's up to you."

"I . . . we'll talk about it. The next time I see her, we'll talk about it."

"Yes," I said. "The next time you see her."

As we walked back to the truck, Hal threw an arm around my shoulder. "You're a regular Miss Fix-it, aren't you?"

Shrugging him off, I said, "I've got problems of my own, not that *you'd* notice."

"Who, you?"

"Yes, me. Mama's worked her fingers to the bone getting me an outfit together to wear to Bernice Ransom's party tonight, and I'm not going. Now I've got to go home and tell Mama. Then I have to call Bernice too. And I'd as soon be dead."

This act seemed to be having its effect, but I went on to make sure. "I guess I'll spend New Year's Eve sitting around in my long skirt watching Aunt Eunice tap her foot to Guy Lombardo on the television. It was over five dollars a yard too."

"What was?"

"The velvet for the skirt, dammit!"

"Oh. Well . . . why aren't you going to the party?"

"You really have had a lot of practice hurting girls, haven't you? Do I have to spell it out? Here's why: BE-CAUSE I HAVEN'T GOT A DATE."

"Oh." Hal looked away from my shame. "Couldn't you . . . couldn't you just go by yourself?"

"Thanks a lot." I climbed up into the truck and banged the door shut. Hal walked around to his side, looking very thoughtful. He was on the hook then. All I had to do was reel him in. The engine turned over and idled. Hal limbered up his hands. "If . . . ah . . . if you want me to, I'll take you to the party."

"Thanks, Hal," I said in a small voice, sounding very sincere.

"Let's not stay too long though, okay?"

"Better than nothing," I said. The truck bucketed up toward the lane. I looked back at the reservoir. In the distance, I thought I heard bells ringing.

chapter

fourteen

*I*t took me the better part of two hours to get dressed. What with fighting my hair to turn up and stay that way and getting that skirt to hang right, I about wore myself out. At the stroke of nine, I started down the stairs, taking it slow for fear those high heels might get into a serious argument with that long skirt tail.

To my mortification, the whole family was gathered down in the hall, looking up. Hal had on his dark blue suit *and* a tie. It's a crime how good-looking that boy is without having to work at it.

But nobody spoke. Just eight eyes watching my descent. "Well, will I do?" I said when I hit bottom.

"You'll do very well," Mama said.

"Very well," Aunt Eunice echoed.

I guess Dad agreed with them, but he just swallowed. Hal stepped forward and offered me his arm. As we left, Mama turned to Aunt Eunice and murmured, "Let's get the spare room ready." I pushed Hal on ahead of me.

Bernice opened her front door and screamed.

"Look at you! Oh, Verna, what did New York *do* to you? You're *fantastic!*" She was jumping up and down. But her mother loomed up in an enormous hostess gown, and Bernice remembered her manners long enough to let us in off the front porch. Mrs. Ransom led Hal into the living room that was already filling up. But Bernice dragged me upstairs. "Any word yet?" I asked her.

"No, not yet, but it's still early." She pulled me into the bathroom and shut the door. Then her whole face lit up in a huge mouth-open smile. I smiled back, of course, but she kept smiling bigger and bigger. I hadn't come to this party to stand in the bathroom and beam at Bernice. Then it hit me.

"Bernice, your teeth. I can see your teeth!"

"Yes! It's all out—the brace, the rubber bands—everything! Except for check-ups I never have to see the orthodontist again! I'm, I'm EMANCIPATED!" We did a little victory dance on the bathroom tiles. "Come on, let's go downstairs," she said. "It's so exciting. It's like we're transformed. You and I and . . . well, come on and see."

"Darlene isn't here, is she?"

"Oh but she is and guess who with?"

"Mysterious, older-man type?"

Bernice giggled. "Hardly. Are you ready for this—Happy Applegate!"

Happy Applegate, the male dingbat of the Dunthorpe

Destroyers football squad? Never. But it isn't like Our Hostess to make up stories.

Big-hearted Bernice had invited half the school. The front hall was thronged with people arriving and departing. Seniors, even, and Beverly Fenster's entire Pep Club. Talk about being in the social swim. The living room was so jammed I could barely see Hal's patient head sticking up above the mob. Mr. Ransom was entertaining him, no doubt with stories of the grocery trade. Mrs. Ransom moved like a battleship through the crowd, carrying a silver tray of individual pizzas.

There was dancing in the room the Ransoms call their solarium. Wade R. Reynolds and Ludmilla were doing their box-step out there. But the minute Ludmilla saw me, she broke from Wade and came straight over. "Say listen, what's the meaning of running off to New York without telling anybody? Good grief, what have you done to your hair? It looks marvelous. And what's come over Darlene? She's lurking behind the Christmas tree like a dormouse. Is that your brother over there? You tell him to come and dance with me. All right, Wade, I'm coming!"

I never said a word.

Suddenly Hal was beside me, juggling a punch cup of something that looked like melted tutti-frutti ice cream. "Are you sure this is a dates-only party? Looks like a lot of singles around to me."

To avoid an answer, I pointed out Ludmilla and mentioned she was yearning for him to cut in on Wade.

"Girl with the firm jaw and the brown dress?" he said. "Maybe later."

Darlene was behind the Christmas tree, where Ludmilla said. Hap Applegate was just leaving her side to lumber toward the punch bowl. She was sitting in a big chair in a prim, long-sleeved knit dress. Without all the liner and shading, her eyes looked a little naked, but she was lovely as ever. Less shopworn too. She looked sixteen for a change.

All the way home on the plane from New York, we'd been—careful with each other. Carefully, I made my way over to her.

"Oh, Verna. Hi," she said, vague as usual.

"Hi, Darlene." Long pause. "Happy Applegate?"

"Well, why not? He asked me. He's been asking me all fall. But this time I said, why not?"

"Sure," I said quickly. "I had to get my brother to bring me."

"You brother can take *me* out any time he wants to," Darlene said sincerely.

"Sorry, Darlene. Not this one. If I had another brother, though, you could have him."

"Thanks, Verna," she said, taking me at my word. "Sit down a minute." I perched on the arm of the easy chair, and there we sat like two badly aligned Siamese twins. Darlene gazed into the twinkling Christmas tree lights so long that I thought she'd forgotten me. "Mother is so mad at me," she said finally, "that she's practically freaked out."

A vision of "Spot the Frauds" flashed through my

head, followed by another one of Mrs. Hoffmeister driving a stake through my heart for publicly shaming her daughter. "Why?"

"Because she said I turned on her. Those were her words."

"Did you?"

"You bet," Darlene said, nodding at the tree. "I told her I wasn't going to Las Vegas and compete for National Super Doll. And I wasn't having her enter me in any more contests or anything. That whatever she thought up for me to do next, I wasn't going to do it."

"Did you mean it?"

"I sure did. I told her she'd have to settle for living her own life and not mine too. And she said so this is the thanks she gets for sacrificing everything and did I suppose for a minute I was going to get any place at all without her doing the thinking.

"Mother's not used to me turning on her. She said I'd given her one of her sick headaches and she'd have to go to bed. And I said that'd be a nice change for her, going to bed by herself for once. Then she came over and slapped me. With her rings on too."

I was shifting around uncomfortably on my perch. This tale of sex and violence was getting a bit sordid. Interesting, but sordid.

"Then I knew it was all right and I'd won. When she slapped me, I knew that."

"I don't think I follow your reasoning, Darlene," I said, meaning it truly.

"Mother never slapped me before. Not with her rings

on. It might have left a bruise or something that would mar my complexion . . . and put me out of the running. She cried one time when I got a fever blister on my lip. I couldn't go on like that, Verna. I just realized that . . . lately."

There was a long silence between us then, though the rest of the party was throbbing away on the other side of the Christmas tree. Through a gap in the drying branches, I caught a glimpse of Moon, in yarn-decorated hopsacking, heading for the solarium. She had a hold on the Biblical-looking college boy she'd brought to homecoming. It was the same old Moon, but it looked like both she and the boy had gotten haircuts. I even heard a scrap from their conversation. Moon said to him, "But I don't *believe* in single-sex liberation. I believe in total *human* realization. When are you going to get that through your thick head, Myron?" I didn't catch Myron's reply.

"What are you going to do now, Darlene?"

"I've been thinking about that. I suppose I better try to pass English. I think I owe Miss Castle seven papers, maybe more."

"She'll probably settle for ten cents on the dollar from you, like the Internal Revenue."

"What?" Darlene turned ravishing, blank eyes on me.

"Skip it. Show her you're making an effort, and she won't lean on you too hard."

"She better not try. Nobody better. Ever."

"I just hated New York," she said. "But I might go

back there someday—when I'm good and ready. If I don't develop any other skills, I might try a career in modeling." She reached out suddenly and took hold of my wrist. "Listen, Verna, nothing personal, but if I ever do go back to New York, I'm not taking you with me."

From anybody else, that might have been a joke. From Darlene, I'll never be sure.

By eleven thirty I was ready to climb the walls, skirt and all. Not that I hadn't been passing the time. Boys I'd been going to high school with right along kept asking me if I was new in town. Finally, I started telling them I was an ex-chicken plucker from Mount Yeomans who'd given it all up for the bright lights of Dunthorpe. Some of them thought that was funny. Some didn't. But they all danced with me.

Everybody was doing close dancing. Except for Moon and Myron who were doing something bumpy and separate left over from the 1960s. Ludmilla never did get Hal onto the dance floor, but I saw she had him cornered in the living room. She was engaging him in deep conversation and blowing smoke in his face.

I was dancing with some guy who was doing his best to trample my feet to bloody stumps when Bernice whisked up and gave me a significant look. I abandoned my partner in the middle of the solarium.

Sherri had arrived. She stood in the front hall waiting as calmly as possible, with a small suitcase at her feet. I'd half expected her to be in her uniform since she'd hitched a free flight out from New York. But she had on a little understated party dress and appeared to have stepped right out of Twenty-seventh Street and up to the Ransoms' door. Did we let her get a word in? I don't think so. Just hugs and subdued squeals. Bernice was bubbling sentimentally, and I, Miss fix-it, was a little anxious.

I led Sherri across the crowded living room, and we approached Hal by stealth from behind. "Okay, Ludmilla, I said around him. "Your time's up. I've got another girl for him."

Hal turned around then, still looking patient. I had the satisfaction of seeing every drop of blood drain from his face. "Verna, you. . . ." he said, but he wasn't looking at me. Just then every bell and siren in Dunthorpe cut loose. The room roared to greet the New Year. Hal and Sherri welcomed it in very much together.

"Come on," Bernice said to me, "let's *us* go find somebody to kiss!"

Ludmilla said, "Has *anybody* seen Wade?"

Early on New Year's morning, Mama, Aunt Eunice, and Sherri must all have arrived in the kitchen at the same time. And you'd think that three women in the same kitchen all trying to put their best foot forward would cause an explosion you could hear all the way to Mount Yeomans. But don't ask me. We'd all been up to the wee hours talking and I overslept.

When I got downstairs, Sherri was just coming in off the back porch in ski pants, a headscarf, and Hal's lum-

berjack shirt. "They're still *warm*," she said wonderingly
about the eggs she'd just gathered. Mama and Aunt
Eunice gave her very tolerant smiles.

I was in hopes Sherri would do us one of her soufflés.
But she was wiser than that. We had our eggs the usual
way, our way. Sherri ate four, over easy. And before
breakfast was over, Aunt Eunice was talking her through
her recipe for boiled caramel cake icing, and Sherri was
listening intently. Dad sat at the table and glowed. And
Hal . . . Hal never had a chance.

"I don't rush to conclusions," Mama said to me while
we were clearing the table, "but Sherri's just like one
of us."

All that morning the kitchen was filled with the smell
of hickory-nut cake baking and the sound of Mama
humming at her chores. Hal and Sherri were out having
such a full tour of the property that Aunt Eunice finally
said she thought they'd probably fallen down the well.

Mama dropped the potato peeler in the sink and turned
on her. "You know what your problem is Eunice? No
boy ever took you down behind the barn!"

"Edith! What a thing to say to me! Why I never!"

"I know you never," Mama said. "That's what I
mean." Then she went on humming, happier than ever.

After lunch, Hal took me aside, looking as sheepish
as I've ever seen him. He was rubbing the back of his
neck and shifting from one foot to the other. I tell you,
it was a joy to see. "Verna," he said, "since you . . . well,
I wanted to tell you first. It doesn't make any sense to

have gone through the whole premed course without . . . what I mean is, I've made up my mind to go ahead and apply to medical school."

I told him I thought it was a very good idea and did he have any other news to tell me? He told me curiosity killed the cat and to get myself bundled up.

"Where are we going?"

"Let's take Sherri out to the reservoir."

"Hal, do you know it's the middle of the winter? What are we going to do out there? Break the ice and swim?"

"Verna, get your coat."

"No, you two go on by yourselves."

I walked them out to the truck, though. And I waved till they were way down the lane, like they were setting off on the longest journey of their lives. Then I turned back and stepped off into the new year, in a direction of my own.

About the Author

Richard Peck was born in Decatur, Illinois. He attended Exeter University, England, was graduated from DePauw University, and received his M. A. from Southern Illinois University. He has taught at Hunter College High School. His recently published novels, *Don't Look and It Won't Hurt, Dreamland Lake,* and *Through a Brief Darkness,* have won considerable acclaim.